The Curse of Knowing

A novel

Aldo Cernuto

Clink
Street

London | New York

Published by Clink Street Publishing 2020

Copyright © 2020

First edition.

ISBN:
978-1-913340-01-8 - paperback
978-1-913340-02-5 - ebook

*To my wife, my children and
my dear mother*

Foreword

Like many readers, I find myself searching for sympathetic or relatable characters when I first start reading a new book. In Aldo Cernuto's novel, we find a character who has an ability to know everything about those she meets. In another story, such an ability would be a kind of superpower, but from this perspective, it is a curse.

When we first meet Vittoria, we find that this curse has taken a toll on her. She is world-weary, pessimistic, and just wants to be left alone. At first glance, our protagonist does not seem all that relatable. She is in her sixties, living in Rome, and suffering from an otherworldly affliction. That said, as I learn more about Vittoria, her past, her present, and her way of thinking, I find myself not only sympathizing with her but also relating.

At some time or other, we have all thought about what it would be like to read someone else's mind. How would that feel? How would it change our lives?

As I wondered why I felt some connection to the plight suffered by Vittoria—the plight of knowing too much—I realized that this is something we all live with nowadays, in some way. A few years ago, I was set up on a blind date. I knew little of this girl except an assurance that we would get along and a single photograph. That was not good enough for me, so I found her on multiple social media platforms and searched for information. I wanted to find things we might have in common, things we could talk about and maybe bond over.

Soon, I found what I was looking for: information on her hobbies, films she liked, and a few coincidences that I no longer had to worry about us discovering by chance. And as I scrolled, I also found a note left on one of her accounts that suggested her mom had passed away just a few weeks before.

This was personal information I wish I had not discovered. I thought about cancelling our date; I now felt her time was better spent without me. But I also worried about cancelling the date and seeming insensitive. We met and, all the while, that information ate away at me. I worried whether she would tell me herself and how I would react. I worried about mentioning my family or asking about hers. I read everything in the context of knowing information she had never told me and had no idea I knew.

We never met again. This is just an example, but, truthfully, we experience such things every day. It is not just the big stuff but the little things. We know what our friends, family, and near strangers have for breakfast, what music they are listening to, and what restaurant they went to for their birthday. We know where they are at all times, we know what they thought of a recent political debate, and we know with whom they are spending time.

We know of their vanity and their need for attention. We know about their petty thoughts, hurtful comments, and frequent nastiness.

This is what Vittoria experiences each day with anyone she comes across. A curse of not just knowing the dark secrets of others but the insignificant too. Over time, the small things become legion and weigh more heavily. With all that noise, all that unwanted information, it is hard to realize that there is a difference between knowing details and truly understanding someone. Vittoria's story is not just about how she became the burdened woman we find her, but about how opening up to love and friendship can change one's outlook and, thereby, the course of one's entire life.

Daniel Bergamini

FIRST

Knowing

ONE

Rome, present day

My name is Vittoria Armieri, I work at the Ministry of Cultural Heritage and I know everything.

If you feel safe, well, you aren't. I know everything about you too, beginning with who you are and what your name is. I can tell where you are right now, what you do for a living and whom you fantasized about just minutes ago.

Like so many of the things that I know about you and anybody else, these are trivialities. These are facts that nobody cares about, least of all me. So, I treat them like gnats that are buzzing around. I wait for them to fly off, without even bothering to wave them away.

But things are different when I come across a murderer, like the guy on the bench opposite. I'm not talking about the older man with thick glasses: he is as clean as a whistle; in fact, he deserves compassion. At age twelve, he was beaten unconscious by three seniors of his boarding school and a year later he was raped by a janitor. He has always kept it from everyone, denying it even to himself. But it happened. I know it did.

Anyway, I was talking about the man sitting next to him, the guy in the blue coat who is now devouring his sandwich. His name is Domenico Morgelli and he's sixty-four. Back when he used to inflict on human beings the same savagery that he's now reserving for his food, he slaughtered a young man and a girl in their twenties. It's no coincidence that he was christened *Dom the butcher* by the whole of Rome at the time of his crime.

I turn my gaze towards the passersby here at Villa Borghese. Unaware of what this guy did, they stroll around the park, looking for some rays of sun in this insipid early autumn. Most of them are employees on their lunch breaks, but I can spot some students too. There's a pair of lovebirds among them. They're crossing the pathway now, preventing me from seeing the murderer for an instant. Their names are Giada and Marcello and they attend medical school. They're both twenty-four years old and have been together for a few weeks. Last Sunday they screwed without a condom; now she is living in anxiety, desperately waiting for her next period. From the way they are holding each other, they seem to have eight arms. Caught by their mutual love, they ignore everyone else, as if they're living in a world confined to themselves.

Yes, that's right: a world confined to themselves.

Oh, how I envy them that!

I dwell on the two lovers. They're walking a few yards from a man who could slice them up, like he did to that couple years ago, and they're practically naked in front of me. But oblivious as they are, they pay no attention to either of us.

As for me, a gloomy and withered figure, I'm not surprised that I go unnoticed by them or by anyone. I see my decay as a conquest, and my desire to hasten it exceeds by far any wish I may have of detaining it. With the misfortune I bear and the stage that I've now reached, my life as an outcast, ignored by everyone, is a blessing.

You wouldn't say it today, but forty years ago anyone would have dislocated their necks to crane at me. The black waves of my hair drank in their gazes like swirls of the sea. Not to talk about my eyes—an out-of-stock hue of blue, as my mother once said; despite being azure they were like two black holes in the way they swallowed the attention of everyone around me. In the summer, when I used to wear a suntan and little else, every step I took was like a whiplash: most people gasped with pleasure; some were eaten up by envy.

But why am I distracting myself with this decades-old nonsense when I'm facing this criminal, who could be just the man for the job?

Meanwhile, the two lovers have moved on, taking the man's gaze with them as he recalls his murder. In 1972, he stabbed both his girlfriend Mirella and Valerio, a young cook who was coming on to her on a park bench on the outskirts of Rome. He ended them with a total of twenty-two thrusts. The first four straight to Valerio's heart. Then, in tears, he delivered the remaining eighteen to Mirella.

But this young couple has no reason to be afraid of him. I've already made a mental note that he served a total of twenty-three years at Regina Coeli for his crime, and he has never thought of committing another one. He wouldn't raise a hand to call a waiter now, let alone kill someone. Other facts I know—he works for his cousin's cleaning company and he has an infection in the lower right third molar, but he can't afford a dentist.

Here's the thing that annoys me the most: irrelevant details sneak stealthily into my consciousness in the same way as significant facts, but I can't choose which to keep and which to discard.

Now the murderer has noticed me and is staring at me. After another bite of his sandwich, he looks away. He can't imagine that this little woman wrapped in a beige coat, with her bag on her knees, knows about his crime. He cannot know, neither he nor anyone else, that I know everything. About everyone.

***

I don't know what the origin of my illness is.

In fact, when I go back in time, in search of a triggering event, it feels like a breath of air is sliding away from my fingers.

Weird, isn't it? I'm damned to know the most worthless details of other people's lives, but not a fact of such magnitude concerning mine. And this is one more reason for me to call it a *curse*.

What I do know, though, is that I lived a quasi-normal existence at a very young age. Until I reached the age of twelve, I felt like any other child, except that I was a bit more reserved and had fewer friends than other classmates. Other than that, my quirks were like everyone else's.

At the time, no one used to call me Vittoria. I was *Vicky* to friends, relatives and acquaintances. I loved being called *Vicky*. I adored the lightness of my nickname. It helped me feel a merry, lighthearted child, with no other thoughts than playing and having fun. In short, the child that I wasn't.

In fact, I was a bit of a crybaby. Seeing someone suffering gave me great pain. And things started getting worse during my second year of secondary school. While my classmates were making friends by the score, I struggled to greet acquaintances. They exchanged their first kisses with boys, but I shied away from them. They laughed and talked to anyone, while I winced at hearing unfamiliar voices. If, all of a sudden, someone spoke to me, I startled like a frightened rabbit.

An early sign of my curse dates back to my sixteenth year. It was a hot summer afternoon when I was coming home from the library. A blonde woman in her fifties stopped me in the street. I remember her northern European accent, perhaps German. She told me that she had lost her way to the hospital and asked if I could help her. The stiffness of her inflection was softened by the warm and persuasive tone. What amazed me was the curious dissonance between her calmness and the urgency that her destination implied. Thanks to her patient expression, I quickly overcame the moment of alienation that I typically experienced when a stranger spoke to me. Her smile, sweet and prolonged, was accompanied by a caring look. She appeared ready to wait an eternity for my answer. Rather than making me anxious, she had released the pressure.

For a long moment, the hustle and bustle of the city seemed suspended in time, as if suddenly immersed in oil. The woman was wearing a large cotton dress with thin multi-colored stripes, very fashionable at the time. With the sun high in the sky and its rays also slowed down, it seemed to me that she was wrapped in a rainbow of cloth. Suddenly, her figure began to lose consistency. For an instant, her whole body evaporated to turn into colors, so many colors, of countless shades, and each had a familiar meaning to me. I can't say how much time passed between the answer I had in mind, namely that I did not know where there was a hospital, and my actual reply with the precise directions to reach it. The immediacy between thought and word, so natural to every human being in a good state of health, was also submerged in that bath of oil. Replaced by notions I didn't know I possessed.

The woman thanked me, touching my arm with a caress. Then she walked away without looking back, and I continued on my way. After a hundred yards, maybe even less, I started thinking that I had sent her down the wrong path. Of course I had. I thought I must have misled her, as I didn't know about any hospital nearby. I then retraced my steps to the place where I had met the woman. From there, I followed the directions I had given her. Walking along unfamiliar streets, I eventually found myself in front of a hospital, which I was seeing for the first time. I was tempted to enter and find the woman again, but I gave up. I thought I'd guessed the route by pure chance— or, for all I knew, I had recovered a forgotten memory.

Years later, with the occurrence of new and increasingly severe episodes, I often thought again about this encounter. For a while, I cultivated the fairytale idea that someone had put a spell on me, just to delude myself that one day I would recover at the touch of a magic wand. In the following years, though, my naive hopes gave way to more logical assumptions, and I started to believe that there had been no first event whatsoever. I convinced myself that I'd been born with my illness. It had remained dormant for most of my youth, only to become more and more invasive over time. Today, aged sixty-five, I have no faith that I'll ever find a cure. I have also lost hope of a stable course. On the contrary, I feel that my symptoms are getting worse day by day. The lives of others break into my consciousness with increasing frequency, while details become more and more precise. Other people's emotions, especially the strongest ones, invade me with such violence as to overwhelm me. I avoid any large gatherings: meetings, concerts, crowded squares, metro queues, museums clogged with tourists. At peak times, I even stay away from the local markets.

One morning, two months ago, I was walking along Via Bocca di Leone and I came across a student rally. They had left Piazza di Spagna and were heading for Via del Corso. To maneuver the narrow streets of the area, their procession had forked between Via Condotti and Via Borgognona. Stuck as I was in the middle of the rally, I had no escape. In an instant, the din of young and intense lives turned into colors. Infinite colors of blinding vivacity that began to swirl around, until they collapsed in absolute darkness. I awoke to the wail of the ambulance siren. A moment later I was being laid on a stretcher. In such situations, other people's emotions no longer reach me one at a time. They lose their individuality to become a shapeless mass, whose physical substance hurts me. Colors turn into matter. They wrap themselves in a solid wave that culminates in an explosion of black. When the impact overwhelms me, throwing me to the ground, the pain is excruciating.

Today, sitting here in the park with a few people around, I can stand the blow. Of course, the vicissitudes of others are annoying and invasive. I feel them jostling nervously around me. I feel their stinging urge to slip into my consciousness. But I can manage them. Although they hit me like a hailstorm along an unsheltered road, I can tolerate them.

My only refuge lies in nothingness. The void is my panacea. Void of color, of life, of souls. And of memories. Even a photograph on a shelf, or a forgotten letter in a book can attack me with emotions I don't seek, nor would I want to know. My sanctuaries, the *terra franca* where I finally find peace, are closed and unadorned rooms, or deserted places, if I could just find some.

But when I come across a murderer, someone like this Morgelli, I bless the moment. Rather than looking for shelter, I stand fearlessly in front of him, trying to dig into his past life. I have to work up the nerve, because the violent emotions, the memories of bloody episodes, are those that strike me the hardest, and, in the end, they leave me drained. But at least I can create an advantage and kindle a hope.

I return to observe the man on the bench for a few seconds. I close my eyes, keeping his image in my memory. It shrivels up, as if about to implode. Then it suddenly tears and blazes up in a forest of colors. It takes on iridescent shades and nuances. They are colors, but to me they mean acts, names, dates and places. I do not see images, yet I see. I don't hear sounds, yet I hear. The man is transfigured; he's young; covered with blood; kneeling; he cries. The data comes to me in succession, with an irregular flow, which I cannot control or interrupt.

I feel them like waves of a malign and violent orgasm, a harbinger of pain. The only pleasure, if you can call it a pleasure, is feeling that it's approaching the end—the flow begins to diminish, and fades away, slowly. Until it disappears.

Then, a last piece of information comes, faint like a watercolor: the most recent detail of this man's life. I feel, without seeing it, that he has stood up. He's watching me.

I open my eyes and in fact there he is, motionless, three yards from me—Domenico Morgelli. I memorize his image and lower my eyelids. He's wondering whether we know each other. He's now rating my age. Then he scrutinizes me again, looking at my clothing for signs of my social status. He's considering whether I might have had a role in his trial, held here in Rome in April 1981. He wonders whether I may have been a member of the jury.

As I raise my face to the sun, I feel his gaze insist on me. I have no fear of him, and I have a thousand reasons for having none.

***

I'm looking for someone to execute me; that's the ugly truth. I have focused my hunt on experienced killers, in the hope of finding someone who will cut short my life too. In other words, I'm in search of an armed hand (or even unarmed, provided it's murderous) that turns me, Vittoria Armieri, or Vicky if you like, into good fuel for a crematorium.

I have plenty of reasons for craving death, as you'll soon realize. There are so many of them, and so valid, that I struggle to establish a priority.

Obviously, my curse is high on the list.

I wish I could find a murderer for that part of me alone, while saving all the rest, as a surgeon does when removing a tumor. Unfortunately, such a specialized criminal doesn't seem to exist. Same for a doctor: no surgical compendium includes the partial or total excision of human-life receptors. My illness is not recognized by science: how could there be a therapy? Since there is no scalpel for the diseased part only, I look for a knife that will sever the whole thing.

I'm not that picky, though: guns and bare hands would do the trick as well. I just need someone who knows how to make good use of them.

My dream is of a serial killer. With such a criminal, the chances of success should multiply. Finding one of them out of prison is quite hard, though. And those I've come across, have proved themselves utterly disappointing.

A few weeks ago, as an enthusiast of medieval art, I entered the Tre Fontane Abbey. Knowing it was semi-deserted, I had decided to immerse myself in its Cistercian stillness. When I entered the church, a mass was underway, attended by a handful of people. To avoid bothering anyone, I took a seat on an empty and secluded pew. After a few minutes, when the priest called for the *exchange of peace,* a man, all hunched over, moved from two rows ahead to shake my hand. His burden of emotions was so heavy that, at the moment of releasing his grip, I thought I would fall unconscious. That guy had already slit three people's throats and was pleading for God's help not to kill a fourth. I could have stopped him at the exit, as to offer myself as an easy prey to his murderous temptations and, at the same time, perhaps save another life. But his contrition was sincere: his current dream was to get locked in a cell of that same monastery, wearing a habit and holding a rosary until his dying breath. If I had followed him, I would have only wasted my time.

Sometimes, especially on Saturday mornings, I slip into a bar near my home, a few steps from the Rebibbia prison, and wait for some fresh ex-inmates to come in. On the unlucky days, which is most of them, it is frequented only by small-time criminals like pickpockets or drug dealers. That depresses me. Worst of all, however, is when I come across the innocent; people who have spent decades in prison for no reason. More than being sad for their fate (everyone has their own), I feel irritated by the time I waste. I root around for a while into their pasts, but the most heinous fault I find, at the best of times, is that they once slapped their wives.

When I manage to identify a *soft subject* (a thug, of course, but who yields to my expectations), I glue myself to them for hours. Sometimes, if I find one of them in front of me, I stare at him boldly, hoping he will meet my challenge. So far, though, I've only managed to get some angry jibes, like: *You old shit, why the fuck are you watchin' me?*

One evening three months ago, at the metro turnstiles, the man of my life, that is of my death, which is just the same, had slipped behind me. His name was Giovanni Buccelli, a brute of fifty-eight years obsessed with old—and preferably ugly—women. Sentenced to eighteen years in prison for killing two of them, he had got away with the murder of his wife, whom he had thrown under a train. This last crime, especially, had ignited my hopes. When I got to the platform, I began to stare at him. I stood at the edge of the safety line. He was only five feet from me. All he had to do was extend his arm at the arrival of the train, and the thing was done. But he did nothing. We both got onto the same carriage, then he got out at my stop, following me for a long stretch along a dark alley. When I heard him come beside me, I expected a knife to suddenly appear, or, better yet, I hoped to feel it slip between my ribs, its tip straight to my heart. Instead, that guy just asked me, with irritating kindness, if I wanted to sleep with him.

That's why I'm pissed off with these two-bit hoods: making them take out a knife or a gun seems an impossible task, but they're always ready with their fucking dicks.

I shouted to him that he should have rotted in jail, paying for killing his wife as well. I told him to immediately disappear from my life, which he did in a flash. Then I regretted it, because clearly he'd wondered how I knew about his past. And this is so dangerous. My wish is to be killed, not pointed at as a witch.

Returning to the man of earlier today, this Domenico Morgelli, I'm now certain that I failed with him too. He has killed two people, that's true, but it happened almost forty years ago. Since then, he's lived like a saint. And here is the problem: this man is completely useless to my purpose. Volunteering for the Red Cross could help him atone for his sins, and it will be useful to the people whose lives he saves, but not to someone like me, who just yearns to expire.

I know what's going on in your mind. I know what's going on in anyone's mind, so how can you possibly hope to escape me? You're wondering why I bother hunting for a murderer when I could throw myself off a bridge (here in Rome there are plenty), or under a train, and end it there for good, instantly. But then there are another couple of questions that come first. I could have used this curse of mine to become some kind of almighty potentate—rich and powerful, right? So why am I, at sixty-five, a humble worker, living alone in a two-room flat on the outskirts of Rome, just longing to be dispatched?

Rummaging through people's lives, I have learned to refrain from hasty judgements. Mind you, that's not for ethical reasons. What principles could I champion? Not unlike Morgelli, I caused the death of two people. Not just any two people, by the way: the two I loved the most.

The fact is, precipitate judgements always lead to wrong conclusions.

Listen to someone who knows everything: either you have all the information or shut up. So, before you step into the shoes of a judge, listen to my full story.

Listen from the beginning, though.

And all the way to the very end.

TWO

1977 – April to June

If my ability to get into people's heads and grasp their secrets has left you open-mouthed, it's only because you have no idea what I was like as a young woman. My beauty was way more prodigious.

At that time—I was in my early twenties—I didn't need to discover the thoughts of people, and, in particular, what was going on in the heads of men. Guys blurted it all out. They were so ecstatic to be in my presence that, to overcome silences and embarrassments, they instantly dispensed with their inhibitions. As a result, they spoke freely and unreservedly, even at the cost of talking nonsense.

Back in those days, my illness manifested itself occasionally, and I used to consider those desultory phenomena nothing but an overactive imagination. Instead of giving them relevance and sensing the dangers, I treated them as natural extensions of my mesmerizing allure.

I know I might appear arrogant, if not obnoxious, by insisting on how beautiful I was at that time. But you'll soon understand that it's for the sake of truth, and not for pride. Vanity never took hold of me. In fact, up to the age of twenty, I did everything I could to remain in the shadows. I scoffed at the philanderers and shunned the compliments of the adulators. I even neglected my appearance to evade their drooling glances. I often bundled myself up in clumsy and unfashionable clothes to avoid jealousy amongst my group of friends.

My third year of university, however, marked the peak of my desirability. The generosity of nature had extended to my whole figure to such a degree that my modesty ended up stinking of hypocrisy. In other words, I was at risk of serving the envious one more reason for hating me.

Back in those days, I was still living with my parents. A couple so drawn to one another by mutual passion that they saw in conjugal love the ultimate scope of existence. Proud of my slew of full marks, they could only imagine a bright future ahead of me. A graduation with flying colors was now within reach, and a brilliant career a logical consequence. They could start dreaming of a good son-in-law, the necessary step towards a couple of grandchildren—joy for their third age.

In April 1977, my heart bumped into a strapping young man a few years my senior. In one fell swoop, I managed to disappoint everyone: my friends, my many other suitors and, most of all, my parents.

His name was Antonello and from a physical standpoint he was nothing special, except for his blue eyes, a 6-foot-1 height and two refrigerator-like shoulders: excellent genetic stock fortified by a past as a scrum half in rugby.

Wow, that's really saying something! Weren't you about to say that? I'm talking to you, female reader. In your dreamy little head, avid for romance, you had already pictured a Greek god, right? Have you forgotten what I just said about hasty judgements? Always wait to hold both hammer and nail before hanging the picture on the wall.

Just like the fish, which rots from the head, his skull should have alerted me from the start. Round and perfectly shaven, it was undersized, especially if compared with his robust frame. But it was his chiseled look that challenged the aesthetic canons of the time. An aquiline nose stood out from his face, coupled with a mouth so tiny as to seem squished up. The result was a contemptuous expression—a nasty look that instilled in others that particular form of respect that arises from fear.

As for being undersize, his hands lumped together with his head. Even his penis, miserably, was of the same batch. But I would discover this only after coming across other more impressive members, that dwarfed his in comparison.

I had been struck by Antonello's low voice, which was set to vibrate every organ of mine, and by his wreck-it-all attitude. He seemed to be born holding a little hammer, like the ones to access fire extinguishers. A tool that he was poised to use at all times. You gave him a rule and he pledged to tear it apart. In the pubs where smoking was prohibited (a rarity at the time), he used to light up a cigar with the express purpose of messing with the owner. Same fate for those who didn't take a shine to him. If some guy dared eye me up, he found Antonello's hands at their collar in no time.

His manners of savage-in-the-city impressed me as well. He wore sweaters on bare skin, drove barefoot, always drank from the neck of the bottle and when he ate pizza, he tore it with his hands. His sensibility for culture clashed with his bearish habits. Just to give you an example, he used to devour the works of Beckett, Ginsberg, Bukowski and the like; after finishing each book he passed it to me without uttering a comment. As if to say *read and learn, woman.*

As an enthusiast of theater, his favorite subject at university, Antonello dreamed of knocking down both its scenic conventions and its physical walls. He talked about improvising plays in the public squares, with actors recruited on the spot. He suggested that cultural associations gave passersby free coupons for buying books to persuade them to watch the shows. "Let's give the people the culture that football has stolen from them and the whole country will benefit from it," he used to say, with solemnity.

He spoke little and listened even less, but for almost any word he had a precise gesture. There's one in particular that I remember. When I happened to speak eagerly to him about an idea that I had come up with, he used to keep his head down, as focused on other issues; then, all of a sudden, he would interrupt me, showing his open palm and rotating his forefinger, two or three times, to invite me to repeat my last sentence. And I would start again from there, in desperate search of the best words to make myself understood.

One evening in late May of 1977, Antonello and I went to dine in a crowded and noisy trattoria at Trastevere. His powerful voice dominated the Romanesque chatter in the background, as if he wanted to shut them all up. Colors, voices, and cries were coming from all around us. So many candle lights were pinching my eyes. The surrounding chaos was about to explode in my head. I could barely understand a word out of three of what Antonello was saying. But the one thing I understood was the one I cared about the most. He was proposing that we start a life together. He had only hastily hinted at that possibility, because the issue at stake, that night, was rather the kind of business he wanted to start up. The gist of the conversation was how we would make a living, and its essence was his career. But, in love as I was with love, I retained from his speech what best crowned my infatuation for him—the promise of a nest where our hearts would vibrate in unison.

His business project, on which he had long dwelt, slipped away from my head like a lock of hair in the wind. What I loved in his project wasn't so much the idea of making money but starting a life together. And, later, even a family. I didn't even consider an alternative path—with money as our main goal. I had always thought that love is the source of all that is good, never vice versa. Just as a torrent always goes down a mountain, and not the other way around.

Antonello's plan, in short, was to earn our living by holding acting classes. During his three years at the School of Dramatic Arts in Bologna, which he often defined as *enlightening*, he had acquired a good theoretical basis of directing and acting. His only practical experience dated back to August, two years earlier, when he had formed with other students a small company—five amateur actors performing along the Adriatic Riviera. Their stage was the beach, and the hapless sunbathers were their audience. They didn't make much money with their show, but some local newspapers were intrigued by the foolishness of their project. Antonello, co-protagonist of the play, had stolen everyone's thunder in the various interviews, earning himself the role of leader. These are all facts that I had learned through a patient collage of his cut-up phrases, which he used to drop into our conversations. He indulged in more articulate narratives only when he found himself among new acquaintances. On those occasions, smelling the scent of a public all for himself, he became garrulous. In those narrations, all of a sudden, their performances on the beach became epic, their audience in shorts and bikinis immense and ecstatic. With entire crowds of half-naked holidaymakers clapping like crazy. Antonello's self-confidence in front of strangers, combined with his attitude of a seasoned director, bestowed upon him the aura of a capable master. The more so in an era, the late '70s, in which it was rather easy to undo the shoes of a fresh graduate and slip on those of a fully-fledged teacher.

Going back to the night of Antonello's proposal, towards one o'clock we had remained all alone in the trattoria. Just the two of us. We were seated at a rough wooden table, all badly scored with names, old dates and little hearts—remnants of generations of bygone lovebirds. A candle stub, about to breathe its last, was weakly glimmering halfway between us. I stared at it, resting my gaze on its final gasp. In that moment, I was no longer there. And I wasn't anywhere. A second later, the flame was stirring on a long white candle, which I held in my hand. Around, it was all dark. I moved the candle towards the center of the table. But it was no longer a table. The wood was now smooth, polished, curved at the sides. Stretching out my free hand, I skimmed its surface, until my fingers hesitated at a small ledge. It was cold to the touch and seemingly metallic. I moved the candle to that point, until I saw that it was a cross, at the center of a coffin. I suddenly retracted my hand, as if burnt, while Antonello's theatrical voice sucked me back into the present.

"We'll start the school in September. We've just three months to get ready."

Tiredness, I told myself. I must just be a bit tired.

"Certainly," I smiled, regaining presence. "I'm ready, I'm looking forward to it, *amor mio*."

When I went back home that night, Mom and Dad were about to go to sleep. I greeted them as if they were now two distant relatives and reached my bed, intending that I would talk to them about Antonello's project, which had now become mine too, in a few days' time.

I chose to do it one morning, at breakfast, just before my father left for work. I wanted to avoid at all costs the kind of quarrel that blows up out of impulsiveness and lasts for hours.

I spilled the beans, providing them with all the details of our plan. Into the medley, as if it were a no-brainer, I also put the idea of quitting my studies, to entirely devote myself to the school of theater.

My enthusiasm collapsed into their silence: they looked at each other, as if in search of whom would speak first. With disarming slowness, they finished off their morsels. Then, with a definitive gesture, they put down their cutlery as if it had suddenly become infected.

While they remained silent, I felt woozy for an instant, and blamed it on my empty stomach. Anxious as I was to sort things out, I had put aside any physical need. I then decided to pour myself some coffee at least. Rather than breaking the silence, the bubbling of the boiling liquid in the cup seemed to emphasize it. An instant later, as I put the coffee pot back on the table, I thought I had heard my father say something.

Vicky, what are you doing? Do you want us to die?

I will never know whether he indeed uttered these words, whether they came out of my fantasy or whether they were, instead, an effect of my illness. In any case, I spent no time investigating where, or how, that sentence had originated. I thought, however, that this might be how parents react when faced with news like their child's sudden decision to leave. I also had the idea that maybe such situations, rather than killing parents, would end up healing them, because in the end they'd understand that their life goes on as before, if not better.

My father suddenly got up and walked out of the kitchen door, while I stayed alone with my mother and her prolonged sighs. A few minutes later, I heard the bang of the front door being closed: my father had left without saying a word. In that instant the sighs of my mom broke into an endless weeping.

At the end of June, about three weeks after informing my parents, I moved out.

Pulling behind me a large suitcase, I left my birthplace to reach Antonello in Tor di Quinto, at the apartment that he had already lived in for a few days. It was a forty-square-meter flat that a friend of his, lured by an unmissable job offer in Brazil, had left for his use free of charge. We had just to pay the bills and that was it. With the money that Antonello had put aside, plus some savings of mine, and almost a year of rent already paid in advance, we had enough reserves to launch our new venture.

A couple of hours later, I was pushing my heavy luggage into the cramped lift of the new house. Right after closing the little doors behind me, I went to press the button for the seventh floor, ready to take off with my dream of love. At that moment, in sudden amazement, I came upon my image in the mirror. At a glance, it seemed that my beauty had fallen a notch. It was the slightest degree, but it was evident. It was a teeny sign of decline, which only I myself could perceive, just as you, and nobody else, will spot your first white hair. Yet, a fraction of my splendor, however minimal, had suddenly flown away. It was as if a hand had snatched it from me somewhere along the way from my parents' house. It took nothing for me to get rid of this feeling—just the time to avert my eyes from the lift's mirror. I thought of it as a sign of stress. I still sensed on my conscience my parents' distressed mood. Their pitiful looks had followed me far beyond their front door. I had felt them weigh on my shoulders as I descended the stairs and then, through my room's window, to the bus stop. After that, calcified in my memory, their sorrow had escorted me all the way down to my new home. That is, right into that lift.

A sudden bump advised me that I had reached the seventh floor. Without even realizing that I had pressed the button, I was already at my destination. As I dragged the suitcase into the tiny apartment, I saw that Antonello was frying an omelet in the open kitchen. A sudden flutter in my heart erased all my worries.

I closed the door and in just half a twist of my neck I got a grasp of the whole flat. From the entrance, I could see the feet of the bed. It was unmade, and the sheets were all wrinkled, as if they had never experienced the sweet caresses of an iron. I moved my gaze towards Antonello, who was dishing up his omelet onto his plate. I thought that all my tensions would soon dissolve into his passionate embrace.

Tension. I thought that it had been nothing but tension. It took many weeks, and several new events, to give a name to what was going on. Provided that a word exists that can deliver the idea.

THREE

Rome, present day

It's almost two o'clock in the afternoon, and I'm now going to leave my quiet bench at Villa Borghese to head to my workplace, at the Ministry of Cultural Heritage. Taking a break from my painful story can only do me good. In the goblet of my life, in fact, there is so much poison that when retracing its course, I must carefully ration the dose of every moment.

As I'm inviting you to follow me, and not just in my narrative but also physically to the place where I work, I'd rather spare you unpleasant surprises. Just because you, unlike me, have no access to the minds of others, this is not a good reason for me to tell you fibs. When I said that I work at the Ministry, I missed out a tiny detail about my job: I'm in charge of cleaning the toilets. Should I feel guilty for omitting that? Well, no one knows more than me how many secrets, even the most vapid tidbits, people keep to themselves, to appear better than they really are.

Without ever lying, I could tell you plenty of falsities. For example, that at my job I occupy several offices (in a way, each toilet is one). Or that I don't report to anyone (how could I possibly report to someone, if no one speaks to me?). Or, again, that I always have the upper hand (the one holding the broom). And, finally, that everyone bows down before my work (no need to explain this one, right?). I could tell you all that, and who knows how much else, always hovering between lie and truth, between the reality and the perception that I'd rather offer. That's what everyone does when the concern for being judged by others exceeds the fear of being exposed. Or when the condition that you want to conceal is so miserable that it's worth the risk of public disgrace.

But since I have nothing to hide, I won't tell you lies, just the truth. It's a fact, for example, that during my time at the Academy of Fine Arts I passed eighteen exams, twelve of them with full marks. Although in the end I didn't get a degree, today I'd have an easy ride with people who have worked here at the Ministry for years, perhaps with important assignments. People who can't tell a Giotto from a Mantegna or a De Chirico from a Duchamp. So, you're now asking yourself how I ended up cleaning toilets. My answer is that another job would force me to relate to others. I would have to share with them ideas, projects, timing. Or even just a physical space. And that's just not possible.

Sometimes I try to imagine myself in a job of higher rank. The result is that I immediately run to seek refuge in my beloved lavatories. For example, there is a very small office, here on the second floor, where just two people work, Olivia and Joanna. Right, just like the de Havilland sisters, but they—on a par with you, maybe, have no clue who these two were. However, Olivia and Joanna's only duty is to scan maps of various museums and organize them into files. I'm talking about special scans: they often have to start from medium-size originals, if not large. No great technical skill is required, though: a training course would make anyone an expert in a matter of weeks. There is a particular reason for me to single out their office. Because it's just the two of them, their need for human interaction is minimal. They could even ignore each other if they wished to, limiting themselves to a quick hello to the colleagues who bring the paperwork to be scanned. But Olivia and Joanna are in fact great friends. While performing their job, they make a lot of jokes, most of which are funny. They carry on their work with such lightheartedness that they finish their shifts as fresh as they began. In their private lives, they often hang out together, also with their husbands. Their kids, two teenagers stoned at all times, are best friends. All of this is possible thanks to the most extraordinary endowment of humankind—the faculty of blessed ignorance to the minds of others. But what if both Joanna and Olivia lacked this precious gift? Well, in this case Olivia would be privy to the fact that Joanna masturbates at least once a week fantasizing about sex with her friend's husband. Joanna, on the other hand, would be aware that Olivia loathes her son, whom she considers a spoiled brat. One would also be acquainted with the size of the other's paycheck. So, the one who earns less, that is Joanna, would realize that Olivia got the increase after she slept with their boss. Joanna and Olivia, eventually, would become cognizant of the other's plot to take his place as soon as he retires. If you can fancy the discomfort of such a situation, where each of the two women knows the pettiness and hypocrisies of the other, prepare to be surprised: I would take it all in my stride. I'd probably feel like I'm reborn. At least, we'd be on a par. We would know that we both suck, so no harm done. In fact, we could even have fun competing over which of us is worse.

Instead, I'm alone in my misfortune. Knowing all about the lives of others, while they ignore mine, means that I have to dissimulate all the time. I must pretend to ignore their badness, envy and betrayals. Or to know their plans to exploit me and maybe annihilate me. It means I have to make a good face to insincere friendships, false flatterers, treacherous suitors, manipulative colleagues. A good sample of human shames. Of course, everyone knows that meanness exists and that it's always around them. But they (other people) can at least lull themselves into the illusion of being loved, or esteemed. On the contrary, I have no escape. Sadly, I live each and every hypocrisy at the moment it is conceived. I suffer every dishonesty as it is accomplished and the evil even before it is done.

For this reason, the toilets are my holy place. The daily duty of cleaning them is a personal ablution from the filth of the planet. A private catharsis in a public place. When my shift starts, I place the little yellow cone down on the floor and indulge in solitude. Locked in the loos, absorbed in my solitary sanitations, I hear the same sounds and silences that reverberate in empty churches. I listen to the echoes of a distant trickling, while mystical creaks alternate with periods of quiet that seem to disperse into the infinite. And I, the sacristan of the temple, walk among the open and desolate stalls; similar to confessionals, but free of sins and sinners. And, especially, of priests.

The toilets, where people close in their shames, are the place where I find shelter, so as to leave them out. You do understand why I feel relieved when I'm here all alone, don't you?

Now, since I feel much better, where did I leave off in my story?

FOUR

1977 – July to early December

If our dinner at the trattoria had been, in some ways, the *ouverture* of our school of theater, the search for our premises was its first official act. Antonello and I spent the whole month of July scouring the area around Viale Tiziano, in the Flaminio district. Although at walking distance from our proletarian building in Tor di Quinto, this part of Rome embodies the cultural spirit of the city. What better place—we thought—for a school of theater?

To save money on the agency fee, we had decided to knock on all the doors of the houses we loved. In addition, we often stopped passersby along the streets, asking them if they knew about any vacancies. Each night, we came back home flushed, exhausted, and discouraged. Sometimes we had a good laugh, though. This one guy, for example, was determined to show us his *atelier workshop* at any cost. The day we went to the appointment we found that it was nothing more than a damp, windowless cellar. As he switched on the light, a couple of rats wriggled their way up to the junk furniture amassed against the wall. But he said that once we got rid of all the stuff, the place would breathe fresh air once again.

After several depressing surveys, we finally found the location that seemed to be just waiting for us. It was in one of the poshest areas of the neighborhood, right beside a small street of pastel-colored houses that somehow recall Victorian architecture, and for this reason is named *Piccola Londra*. The façade of the building, a prestigious *palazzo liberty*, was an impressive spectacle. Yet, as we passed the front door, our expectation faded into temporary disappointment: to reach the premises we had to cross the entire courtyard, zigzagging over some decrepit tiles, then go down a half-staircase and pass through a little metal door. But once inside, there was so much space that every fantasy could get lost, find itself and get lost again.

It was love at first sight. The final and most decisive of Cupid's arrows hit us, though, when we learned that the premises belonged to a charitable association. As such, they were morally obliged to keep the rental price low, refraining from the typical greed of most landlords in Rome.

Years before, the place had housed a mechanical workshop, as evidenced by some abandoned machinery and, especially, by the graphics on the walls. One of the writings, *OLIO MOTORE*, ran for about ten yards along a wall. Although barely legible, it was incredibly beautiful. It was my idea, at that point, to bring the place back to its original character. With that in mind, we spent a good part of August working hard at our *conservative restoration*. After three weeks of exhausting brush strokes, the workshop had regained its original appearance. But with a hint of cartoonish flair. To bring out the writings of the fascist era, in fact, we had used strong and saturated colors, reinforcing their outlines with overpaint. Once we had mounted a platform in front of the writing, we realized that, lo and behold, we now had both a stage and a theatrical set. It didn't take a great leap of creativity to christen the place *The Theater Workshop*.

By the beginning of September, after we had had several stacks of flyers printed at an adjoining copy-shop, we were disseminating the dream of becoming an actor throughout Rome.

The first to show up was Emilia, a retired teacher who admitted she was undecided between a theater school, like ours, and a series of sessions with a therapist. Finally, we managed to convince her that she would have more fun with us.

A month after opening, we could count a dozen members. They were mostly dreamers, men and women, of all ages. Some were university students, some former teachers, but others were just workers and employees. They were all ready to sacrifice their time and money in the name of a sacred idol of that era: free creative expression. We were making very little profit ourselves, but Antonello seemed to have finally put down his destructive hammer to start building something. The confidence to make it was within reach.

While new students were constantly approaching the school, the early birds were now becoming familiar with the place. Not just with acting, but also among themselves, and consequently with Antonello, their undisputed mentor. The most enthusiastic among them used to stay until late at night, absorbed in endless conversations, while some others were already launching ideas for an amateur performance. Two students, Sonia and Rodolfo, among the first to enroll, had fallen in love and now were about to put on stage, but as an official act, their marriage. Meanwhile, a group of seasoned amateurs, mostly former teachers pulled in by Emilia, our first student, was now spiraling. One of them, Demetrio Pistolesi, a professor of Greek, had rewritten Sophocles' *Antigone* in comic form, and now wanted Antonello as artistic director. Pistolesi's idea was to recruit other actors among the young at heart, to organize a charity play in his old school. Antonello feared that such a hubbub would make a mockery of his role, jeopardizing the reputation of the school altogether. At the same time, they were a large group, and we were money hungry. Antonello decided to create a session dedicated to the *Epigone di Antigone* (this was the title chosen by Pistolesi), and to relegate it to Friday evenings, well away from the other courses.

As for me, I was a character in search of a role. Now that the school no longer needed a decorator, or a graphic designer for promotional material, and very seldom a flyer distributor, my full-time activities had focused on accounting and housekeeping. From the students' perspective, I was nothing more than the director's bimbo. Indeed, given Antonello's reluctance towards soppy stuff in public, they saw him as my boss, and me as just an airhead infatuated with his charm. Infatuated to such an extent as to consign myself to him both as gofer and mistress. I used to smile about their speculations, but when I was looking for Antonello's reaction, I always found in his dark attitude more confirmations than denials of my lowly status.

Everything went smoothly for over two months, until mid-November, when a sharp quarrel between Antonello and Pistolesi led to the cancellation of the *Epigone di Antigone*. As a result, the session for the older amateurs was terminated.

The incident happened on a Friday night, during a rehearsal. Pistolesi wanted to give the acting a clownish turn, and Antonello had opposed with a firm refusal. Raising his voice, he had put a stop to the laughter of the group, more interested in telling jokes than rehearsing their lines. It took nothing to go from tough talk to threats, and, finally, to outright pushing and shoving. At that point Antonello grabbed Pistolesi by his arm, dragging him out into the yard, as if to settle accounts. The flock of the actors, divided between peacemakers and fistwavers, thus witnessed a violent exchange of slaps, with Pistolesi soon on the ground, bleeding from the lip. A few minutes later, the indignant crowd swarmed out. On leaving, a couple of them were ranting vocally, threatening to go to the police. Predictably, no one in the group showed up at the next class, nor set foot in the school again.

It would not be fair to say that I took sides with Pistolesi's group at that moment. Although I was shaken by the scene and disgusted by the violence, I thought that Antonello had done the right thing, protecting the school's good name.

Just a few minutes later, however, another incident occurred. Although less severe than the fight, it produced the first crack in my covenant of devotion to Antonello. We were about to leave the school to get back home. Just before turning off the lights, Antonello realized that one of the old guys, in his hurry to leave, had forgotten a linen vest. While I was closing the little door with two turns of key, he fumbled quickly inside the pockets of the vest, but found nothing. Upon reaching the other end of the courtyard, where the trash bins stood, he opened one and threw the vest into it. I noticed a gesture of fierce malice and a flash of cruelty in his eyes, as if he wanted to take out, on that poor garment, a beating that in his view hadn't lasted long enough. Then, with that nod of his, he bade me follow him, and we walked home.

Over the next few weeks, which ran quietly, new students arrived at the school, almost all young. The Friday night slot, which had remained vacant after the unpleasant incident, was soon filled by a class of brilliant debutants, a receptive audience to Antonello's stentorian voice.

Meanwhile, the youngest students had somehow renamed the Theater Workshop, deciding to simply call it *The Workshop*. Not only was it shorter, but they had thus made it their own place—a base for studying and meeting of which they felt proudly part. *See you at the Workshop* was the most common expression in their arrangements. And others gradually became more frequent: *I joined the Workshop; we met at the Workshop; what shall we do after the Workshop?* Small hints that Antonello's intuition, though as yet unaccomplished, was beginning to make headway.

Thus, early December rolled around. It had been a week of intense coming and going at the Workshop, with many people inquiring about January's sessions. Many of them were driven by sheer curiosity. However, counting both the students and patrons in search of news, there had been days when the place resembled more of a crowded foyer than a theater school.

One Friday evening of mid-December, the students had grilled Antonello with a barrage of questions about Stanislavski's acting techniques, and he had made himself available to their curiosity. When we left the Workshop, it was past midnight. Antonello and the students walked to the exit, while I, trembling from the cold, was struggling to locate the keyhole of the little metal door.

Once outside the building, we stopped for a few more minutes on the dark sidewalk before everyone took their own paths. We were stomping our freezing feet, but we made time to exchange a few last words. It was at this moment that it happened.

Antonello took out the matches to light up a cigar and enjoy the last puffs of that long day. Just as the flicker of the flame illuminated his profile, I turned to him. I saw him wrapped in a sudden blaze. I somehow felt the smell of burning, sensing the heatwave on my body, that was actually numb from the cold. It was as if a sacrificial brazier had ignited, with tongues of amber fire rising above his head. It lasted a blink of an eye, with the flames immediately sucked back into the darkness of the night.

The image that had formed in my mind, however, was crisp and persistent, as if it were to stay there for life. In front of me, I saw nothing more than Antonello sucking the cigar, but a mental impression overlapped this reality. It showed Antonello in the act of lifting a stick to an elderly woman, as if he were about to beat her.

Following the fate of dreams, which, on our awakening, evade our attempts to catch them, so also disappeared this scene of Antonello holding the stick. A moment before it had seemed indelible, and in the next I doubted that I had ever seen it. The students wished us goodnight with ringing voices and walked away in the freezing night. Antonello and I headed for home. Leaving behind the good-natured attitude he had maintained with the guys on the course, he reverted to the typical roughness of our private moments. Without a word, he started to walk by my side.

Once again, I found an easy explanation in the late hour and in the tiredness I had accumulated. Naive as I was, I came to think that the cause of my strange experience was the countless joints that Antonello and the guys had smoked during the intervals. Dope that I had passively inhaled without even realizing it. That's what I thought on our way back home.

My only desire, at that moment, was to reach our bed and abandon myself to Antonello's embrace. Nothing could get in the way of our dreams.

FIVE

Rome, present day

Welcome to my workplace. Come on in and get the full picture of what I do for a living.

Just don't trip over that yellow cone on the floor. I placed it there as a deterrent, and it's not always effective, however: a lot of people, compelled by sudden urinary urgency, dart into the toilets pretending not to see it. Many of them even leap over the mop that I'm pushing across the floor. I often see them carefully waddling to the loos, the necessary gait for a floor infested with germs. *Better ridiculous than infected*, they seem to think. Which is probably why I have never seen anyone go head over heels around here.

Try and do my job for just a day, and you'll realize what unites all of humanity. Despite separate entrances and different sanitary fittings for each gender, once inside you won't see a big difference between men and women. Same thing with young and old. True equality, far from being celebrated in the parliamentary halls or in the courts, is represented here in the loos. The only distinction that makes any sense around here is whether the urge is to empty your colon or drain your bladder. And that's because I'm lucky enough to work in the toilets of a Ministry, by and large well frequented. Usually, public toilets present a much more assorted collection of evacuations. From pickpockets, who quickly unpack just-stolen wallets, to junkies, who slowly send their lives down the pan. In between, any possible container of human fluids can be emptied. The stomach tops the ranking, followed by the salivary glands and the seminal vesicles. Even infinitesimal receptacles such as clogged pores find their way out, with white dots on the mirrors.

I'm keeping until last, as a category of its own, but also from respect to sorrow, the emptying of lacrimal sacs. Only I know how many people lock themselves in the toilets to pour out their drops of pain. Not that tears leave any trace, to be clear: tears are the noblest of human secretions. Very seldom do they reach the floor. If left flowing down the cheeks, they eventually settle on the surrounding fabrics, absorbed by t-shirts, blouses, or jackets. And many more neckties than you might credit. The distinction between *men who weep* and *real men* may apply to places other than loos. Toilets don't have separate entrances for them. Their doors and walls deserve acknowledgment for letting people be who they want to be. Often, when I see someone locking themselves in, brimming over with tears, I put the broom sideways at the entrance, and I leave them alone with their sorrow. The sensory stimuli typical of these places are not ideal companions for those grieving a death or heartbroken over their cheating spouse. I myself get out of their hair when I see someone enter the loo to cry. I stand guard at the entrance, trying to divert my attention towards other employees. Mind you: not that I care about these. I just use them as distractions, as you would do if the nurses came to wash the neighboring patient in hospital: wouldn't you turn and gaze out of the window, focusing on some tree top or chimney? Same thing I do when I catch someone sobbing in a cubicle. I move my attention elsewhere, towards glimmers of ordinary lives, perhaps insignificant, but useful for my purpose.

Today, at eight o'clock on Friday night, employees and executives have already left for the weekend. It's time for me to attack the women's toilets on the second floor. Right now, I'm pushing all the doors of the stalls in quick succession to open them wide. Soon I'll have to get in with the mop and finding them ready will make things easier. Besides, the open view of the toilets extends the sense of emptiness around me, making me enjoy my loneliness. I hear the doors slam against the partition walls, and that echoing is a hymn to my isolation from the world.

I know that such a mania for a hermit's life is not easy to comprehend, so let me explain it. How many times have you said that your best working hours are those when you're all alone? Do you want confirmation of this? Just imagine that you're at your workplace, with all your colleagues around. Imagine that in addition to feeling their presence, their voices, the ringing of their phones and their frantic movements all around the office, you also intercept their thoughts and memories. Try to imagine yourself overwhelmed by the details of their lives, the ideas they hold about the world, about others, and about you. Could you ever work under similar circumstances? Wouldn't you immediately run for the job of a hermit?

Now, the only living soul in the whole building, I'm sweeping the broom from side to side on the damp floor. In the meantime, I go back in my memory to the Theater Workshop. I must recognize that it's to its credit that I started this job. It was there, as general dogsbody of the school, that I overcame that squeamish attitude of a spoiled child. It was there that, with the help of a glove, I dealt firsthand with dubious encrustations, misplaced pees, and abandoned tampons. At the time, I couldn't possibly imagine that one day this would become my full-time job. In any case, it's there that I started walking the beat.

Precisely there. At that time, and in that place.

SIX

1977 – Mid-December

I didn't want others to see me. That's why I often started my chores at the school late at night, when all the students had already gone. At other times, I used to arrive extra early in the morning, away from any prying eyes, including those of the building's other tenants. More often than not, however, a cleaning shift of the toilet was necessary even during the lunch break. Even then, I took advantage of my alone time for locking myself in and doing the job. In a way, you could measure the success of the school by the number of flush pulls resounding throughout the day, with my workload increasing along with them. The toilet was just a bit larger than a shower tray. There was just room for the water closet and a corner washbasin where you could barely get your fingertips wet. It was the only privy, serving the twenty or so students who dropped by the school every day.

At first, it was tough. I remember one night in particular. One of the kids, probably anxious about the imminent rehearsal, had brought up his pizza over the toilet floor. As a result, I had to clean up my own vomit too.

During that year, I overcame my little idiosyncrasies as the only child, pampered and petted since birth. And I became very efficient. I could often get into the toilet, get it spic and span, and exit in a matter of minutes, four at the most. I then needed two more hours to clean up the main room, which Antonello always wanted flawless. This was the part that bothered me the least, even though on rainy days, with the students constantly tramping back and forth through the courtyard, I had my work cut out in the intervals between lessons. At least once a week, usually on a Saturday morning, I had to dismantle the stage—a rectangle of twelve wooden pallets which we had covered with anthracite carpet. Despite being nailed together, the pallets tended to move, causing the carpet to form wrinkles, ugly to look at and dangerous for the students. Each time, my only option was to remove the carpet and then rearrange the underlying structure. I pointed out to Antonello that if we nailed an intermediate layer of linoleum to the pallets, I would be spared all that trouble. He replied that the students had to *sense* the thumps of their footsteps on the wooden floor, otherwise, instead of a theater, they'd feel as if they were in a gym.

During the lessons, and especially when the rehearsals were underway, I used to sit down at the counter by the wall. It was a legacy of the old workshop—a thick wooden shelf that in its past life had sustained a bulky lathe. There, with my back to the stage, I started the other half of my job: balancing the books, renewing the subscriptions, handling the correspondence. I would also send letters of introduction to high schools and universities, in search of potential new students. It was a menial and tedious task, but since I knew its importance, I handled it with a fair compromise between haste and accuracy. I always tried to finish work early enough to eavesdrop on the final half hour of the class, when Antonello gathered the students in a circle. Sitting at its center, he explained to them the technical features of a stage. His every sentence came to my ears like a wave of pleasure. At first, I was just content to grasp the sound of his words. There was so much wisdom in the sound of his voice. And mastery. No wonder no one ever dared interrupt him. I was fascinated by his way of alternating dry and sharp sentences with prolonged disquisitions. Over time, however, I began to dwell more and more on the content. During this part of his lessons, I often pretended to be absorbed in my job as accountant, completely focused on making ends meet, but I was actually taking notes. I was writing down his precepts, word by word. Meanwhile, I tried to visualize in my mind the equipment and devices of a proscenium, paying the same attention as the students. Unlike them, however, I had to refrain from asking questions, lest I be struck by Antonello's withering gaze.

The subject that enthralled me the most, perhaps because related to my academic studies, was the management of the lighting and its effects on the various materials onstage—scenography, backgrounds, and costumes. I lacked the courage to admit it, but, deep inside, I cultivated the dream of becoming Antonello's assistant one day. Thus, I would have finally put to use my passions for painting, drawing, and photography. Subjects that I originally wanted to combine in my dissertation, with the idea of unifying them into a single discipline of my own invention, which I used to call *reflectance*.

One particular morning, I suggested to Antonello that he build large wooden frames, with a light structure. By mounting on them some colored gauze, in several layers, and working on the lighting, we could create some iridescent backgrounds, breaking up the monotony of the stage. The students themselves, living in an always-changing environment, would find reasons to renew their subscriptions. Halfway through my passionate peroration, which I had accompanied with some sketches, Antonello interrupted me by raising his hand and went to the toilet. Once he returned, however, he changed the subject, reminding me that I needed to pay the electricity bill. Ah, right, and that the toilet paper had run out.

Yet, back in those days, I was still calling it *love*. I used to call it *love* because I needed to give it a name. And a place. Not so much in my heart, which despite my better instincts remained steadfast, but at least in my dictionary. I could also call it other names taken haphazardly from my eclectic vocabulary of the time: *astrolabes*, *palingenesis*, *idiosyncrasy*, *hermeneutics*. All terms I had heard of, getting a vague idea of their sense, but without precise knowledge of what they meant. In the same way, I didn't have a definite concept of love. Identifying it with Antonello himself had been my simplest solution. It was such an absolute equation that it was easy to see in him my savior. I ought not to suffer for his rude gestures, or for his grumpy remarks—I concluded, because that's love. And just because it's love, whatever he does and says must be love too, just like all that he undoes and denies. Therefore, his arrogance was also love. Even his haughtiness. Even his alpha-male attitude. It was all love, and it could only be fantastic.

When we were alone, he treated me just as he used to treat his students: he alternated furious outbursts that shook tears from your eyes with gestures of unexpected sweetness. If, with his pupils, after a rant, he soon switched to a gentle tone, often accompanied by a hug, or a eulogy, with me he served breakfast in bed, with an accompaniment of kisses.

One Sunday morning while we were lounging in bed, enjoying our day of rest, I tossed out the idea of becoming his student. Not that I had in mind a future as an actress—I just wanted to get closer to him, perhaps scoring points for my ambitions of becoming his assistant. To my surprise, Antonello smiled back at me. It was such a wide smile that it seemed to convey enthusiasm. He told me that it was a brilliant idea, and that he would be delighted if I joined the new beginners' course starting the following week. Yet when the day of the first lesson came, he said nothing. In fact, he found an excuse to send me to the post office for an errand. I assumed that he had had an afterthought, and I didn't find the courage to bring up the subject again.

As for Mom and Dad, I kept them at a distance. I was only too aware that my every reason for loving Antonello was a cause of concern for them. So much so that I had ceased to talk about him. I even avoided mentioning his name—an effective strategy to dodge any questions they might ask. In my sentimental world, Antonello and my parents were two separate and non-communicating entities. Keeping them distinct, and distant, was my guarantee for a quiet life. Luckily, Antonello's reluctance to speak about his parents made things easier. Not once had he proposed a trip to Bologna, where they lived, to meet up with them.

There was a sad circumstance that our respective parents shared: we were both their only children and not by their choice. While my mother had undergone a hysterectomy after my birth, a far more serious loss had affected his family. Their eldest son, a paratrooper in the army, had perished during military training in Sardinia. As with many things from his past, Antonello wasn't keen to talk about it. I had to settle for knowing his name—Alessio—and for a picture that Antonello showed me one night. He was a big blond guy with a sunny smile, and his resemblance to Antonello seemed confined to their sturdy builds. He showed me that picture only once, right after dinner, allowing me to hold it in my hands for just a few seconds. Then, without giving me time for a question, or for a comment, he took it back immediately. He slipped it out of my fingers and back into his wallet.

The unhealthy nature of my infatuation with Antonello lay in the fact that I saw only love without grasping its madness. Just one single episode, like that picture snatched out of my hands, was enough for something to become my norm. On another occasion, he would grab from me a pen, a newspaper, a dish towel, or a book. Without my being surprised, nor my resenting it. As a result, Antonello's oddities were sneaking into my life in the most insidious way: through ordinary daily life.

Then there had been the incident of that night, when a sudden flash of fire had revealed Antonello in the act of beating an old woman. While preserving a clear memory of that scene, to the point that I could reconstruct its every detail, I seldom reverted to it. Nothing could be true about that story. The blaze had not happened, this was certain, so everything else had to be a figment of my imagination too. In any case, I thought it out of the question that Antonello could beat an old woman.

Although I was aware of his quarrelsome attitude, I ruled out the possibility that he could be guilty of such violence. Therefore, it must have been a hallucination: what else could it be?

The aftermath of the festive season, at the reopening of the school, made me reconsider that episode.

The abyss was near. No closer to becoming aware of its existence, I was approaching it fast.

SEVEN

Rome, present day

It's ten o'clock at night when I leave the Ministry to head for home. As I pass through the turnstiles, I nod to the security guard and get out onto the street. Standing on the dim sidewalk, I quickly glance left and right and, to my relief, find the street almost deserted.

Breathing in the misty autumn air, I can inhale a little joy too. Perhaps I call *joy* what for others is just ordinary life. Anyway, that's how I feel when I leave work so late at night. The fewer passersby along the street, the more I can keep my head free of their indiscreet emotions.

It makes me smile when I think about how people would react if they knew about this plight of mine. Instead of naming it an *illness*, or a *curse*, as I usually term it, they would call it a paranormal faculty. Or a supernatural power. Wishing they could possess it too.

Admit it: you are thinking the same.

It always amazes me that people can be so shallow and short-sighted about this kind of thing, but I forgive them nevertheless. I understand. The fact is, most people would say that my condition is something from a fairy-tale, impossible in real life. So, they don't waste time evaluating its true nature. People usually can see no further than the trivial and selfish advantages they could accrue: reading the minds of their bosses to advance their careers, winning at poker, exploiting the weaknesses of their enemies, having it easy with girls. And those with even fewer scruples would make it their perfect partner in crime: an invisible and faithful accomplice for blackmail, or the theft of sensitive data from private companies, if not from public institutions. In any case, they would see it as a tool for their own success. No one would ever dwell on the unspeakable misery it engenders.

Anything but a *power.* It would be a power if it were within my power to decide when to exploit it and with whom, including the opportunity—which I would grab in the blink of an eye—of getting rid of it altogether. But reality is far from being so.

Look at the man who is now crossing the street towards my side. He is a plumber. I've met him several times along this sidewalk, always at this time of night. He's fifty, he's married, he has a fifteen-year-old son whom he adores, and who wants to become a champion footballer. This man is as honest as the day is long; he has never been unfaithful to his wife and he regularly pays his taxes. Does he have something to hide? Yes, of course he does, and it's something terrible, but I'm not going to let on. I'd like, first of all, not to know what it is myself. I wish I knew nothing about him, other than that he's a good plumber, so I can call him when I need one.

As I see him approach, I'm tempted to stop him.

"You're a man of integrity," I would say to him, *"a good father, great in your job: this is what really matters in life. What happened to you was just an unfortunate accident."*

"What do you know, you crazy old bat? Mind your own business!" he would yell at me, running away.

I let the man walk by, and I proceed to the subway, where I'm going to run into other painful events, wretched lives that I perceive just one way—a myriad of information that overwhelms me, with no chance for me to deflect it. It's as if you could hear on the phone the cry of pain of the other, but couldn't get through to express yours, or to extend your sympathy. And, worst of all, no possibility of getting off the phone.

I now see a woman approaching on my side of the street. She seems quite young, but her gait is clumsy. As she gets closer, I realize she's a gypsy. When I happen to meet one, and she asks to read my hand, I let her do that. And, in the meantime, I read her life. This woman, however, wears a worried expression. Instead of stopping me, she just throws me a glance and hurries past me. She's looking for her daughter, who yesterday left to go beg and is not yet back at the camp. Even if I wanted to help this woman, I couldn't. I have no idea where her daughter is, and any effort to know would be of no use. How can you possibly call *power* something that I can neither control, nor expand, nor restrict?

Yet, back to Antonello's times, I could have made good use of it. I could have saved people I loved from death, avoiding throwing my life into despair. But at those times I didn't even know what to call this misfortune of mine, let alone spin it to my advantage. How could I ever name, just by feeling an itch, the insect in my hair? Is it a fly? A tick? A bug? How could I say?

And, yes, at the end of the day, it is a sort of a bug that I have somewhere in my head: a receiver, neither electronic nor organic (and I don't know of what nature), which intercepts people's thoughts at its leisure, whether I like it or not. At that time, this bug was so microscopic that I could hardly feel it. Now, instead, it's too massive for me to endure.

Meanwhile, eager to skip the hustle of the people moving towards the subway, I decide to go out of my way: after turning left in Via delle Carine, I sneak along Via del Colosseo, which is devoid of any sign of life at this time of night.

There are times when I enjoy my illness, relishing its unbearable presence. And one of those moments is right now. I'm walking along a dim and deserted street, inhaling my solitude as if it were a vital breath, a scent of existence. Normally a woman of my age would fear unpleasant encounters under these circumstances. She would walk so close to the walls as to scrape along them. But for me it's different. As I fancy running into a possible murderer, I proceed peacefully. Full of hope, I'd say. If I decide to walk against the walls (which I sometimes do,) it's for quite another reason. It's so that I can appear more defenseless in the eyes of a malefactor, and thus a more enticing prey.

I make it to the subway station unscathed, as has been the case for decades, with my resignation. But as I go down the stairs to approach the platform, I prepare for more frightening aggressions. *Lights. Colors. Noises. Sounds. Smells. Words. Cries.* And, what is even worse: *Existences.*

A sundry collection of information that, innocuous for anyone else, is enough to injure me gravely, especially when mixed with moods, memories, impulses and disturbances, heavy chunks of pain and detonating passions. Footprints of souls that flash around me, ready to condense into a painful mass. In fact, when I least expect it, they break down in a wave of deflagrating power, an explosive jumble of pain.

Now that I have reached the platform, I'm anxious for the train to arrive. I look forward to making it to the last carriage, usually the least crowded. And when I finally take a seat, I think to myself that at last the day is over. Today I've made it. True, I failed to die, I missed once again the only goal I have in life. But at least I didn't collapse unconscious on the floor, torn asunder by despair.

EIGHT

January 9, 1978 – Early morning

It was the second week of January. To be precise, it was the first Monday after the feast of the Epiphany. As the alarm clock rang, I threw my whole body upon it to shut it up. I didn't want its ringing, cruel enough to my own eardrums, to annoy those of my sleeping prince too.

For a brief instant, my five-fifteen wake-up call had taken me back to my early years, to the utter shock of returning to school after the long Christmas break. At the time, I had to get up at dawn to finish my holiday homework. Now, though, there was no mathematics to review, nor Latin exercises to quickly fix. The work that awaited me, once I got to the Workshop, would be all about cleaning and organizing. After some general sweeping and dusting, I would fumigate the whole place by dint of scented detergents on the floor. I would then spend at least one hour rearranging the pallets that served as the stage and vacuuming the carpet that covered them. Since I needed a solid session of elbow grease to get the toilet sparkling clean, I would keep it till last.

Later, once I had peeled off the rubber gloves, I would tackle the paperwork, updating the membership cards of the old students and transcribing the data of the new ones. Lastly, I would start the part of the job that I hated the most—the accounts. Expenditures and incomes, once again, would wrestle with each other, with the profits playing the part of feeble onlookers.

The reopening of the school was scheduled for the following day, with a half-yearly course for the intermediate level. This implied a new round of students, probably very demanding ones, to whom we had to present the school at its best. Antonello was always telling me that everything around the stage had to be clean, orderly, perfect. He argued that even the smallest sign of neglect was an element of distraction, both for him and for the students. Nothing could assist him in his job better than shiny, tidy, and irreproachable surroundings. It's for all these reasons that I had decided to get up so early. I yearned for Antonello's approval and I knew that hard work was the only way to achieve it.

As I turned on the stove for the coffee maker, I thought back to the heartache of minutes before, when I had left his warm embrace to get out of bed. Also, I recalled his broad and comfortable chest, which seemed to have established a perfect ergonomic fit with my back. It felt like our bodies, entwined for countless nights, had progressively modeled themselves on one another, and then, thanks to kind and mutual concessions of their respective anatomies, they had finally reached an ideal match.

While waiting for the coffee to brew, I also thought back to the poetry of our recent Christmas break. Away from the stress of work, we had recovered the happiness of our first moments together. The afternoon of Christmas Day was the icing on the cake. That day, to make up for a long-faced lunch with Mom and Dad, I joined Antonello in Piazza del Popolo. The atmosphere all around was warm and enveloping, as if December had suddenly taken a day off from winter. With our jackets thrown over our shoulders, we had walked over to the Pincio Terrace. Although I had already become jaded with that view, this time I had the feeling that I was visiting it for the very first time. As soon as I looked at the immense square from the top, I felt unique in the world. Who else could find themselves in such an enchanting place to enjoy such an intense passion? What other woman on earth could see her hopes of love match so ideally with the reality of life?

These were my sweet thoughts on that second Monday of January. A morning that I'd rather call a night, as it was still pitch dark outside. But there was another memory, much more recent and of quite another kind, that was stirring in my mind—a bad phone call with my mother, just the afternoon before. She had insisted I join her and Dad for dinner, but she had refrained from giving a reason. I had declined by saying that my alarm clock was set at a quarter past five the following morning. Consequently, Mom and I had ended the call on bad terms. This last thought, which occurred just as the coffee maker had started to sputter on the stove, had somehow troubled my awakening. In serving my coffee, I decided that I would call her later in the morning, after my chores at the Workshop.

Lifting my gaze from the steaming cup, I glanced at the black sky outside the window. Only then did I realize that it was snowing. A few faint flakes were banging against the glass. They looked like nocturnal insects that, driven mad by the cold, were seeking shelter inside, finding death instead. I could easily foresee the below-zero temperature that I would find outside. At that moment, with a hint of smug heroism, I identified myself with a worker of the hard times in the aftermath of the war: a mother tried by her harsh life, but proud to challenge it every day. A woman who leaves home heading for the factory, intrepidly, for her early-morning shift. She's probably despondent at the idea of eight hours at the assembly line, but the coziness she will find once back home will be a priceless reward for her sacrifice. So, animated by a spirit of emulation towards that imaginary heroine, I grabbed my puffer jacket and ran down the seven floors two steps at a time, until I darted out of the front door.

Once outside, I found myself completely alone, surrounded by nothing but snow and blackness. With the two-fold purpose of warming my body and chasing away all fears, I hurried along the street at a running pace. Meanwhile, I fantasized about being a sharp knife—a blade that pierces the indistinct mass of darkness and frost and, by splitting one from the other, defeats their alliance: disrupts the former and mitigates the latter.

Meanwhile, a delicate blanket of snow had formed on the sidewalk. Its immaculate whiteness seemed to want to show me the path. At the same time, however, it hid the slippery areas, making the underlying ice treacherous. Several times on my way to the Workshop, I had to regain my balance at the very last moment, until I decided to adopt a more cautious pace.

It was ten to six in the morning when I reached the building, and everything was still wrapped in the darkness of night. Beyond the main door and past the hallway, I found a soft mantle of snow in the inner courtyard as well. Tracing some footprints that dotted along the path, I made my way to the metal door of the Workshop. Just as I was struggling to slip the key into the latch, I perceived a presence behind me, and, with a thrill of fear, I recalled those traces in the snow. In that very instant I felt a hand on my shoulder, while a familiar voice softly spoke my name. Terror and reassurance broke over me simultaneously. Opposing feelings that, instead of cancelling each other, redoubled my agitation, making me startle. The touch on my shoulder had been soft, like a gloved hand, while the voice, which was warm and deep, sounded intimately familiar. Gasping in disbelief, I turned around and found my father standing before me. He stared at me with a steady gaze, but his mouth worked continuously, as if afflicted by a nervous tic. At that moment, I blamed the cold. I instinctively hugged him, eager to protect him. I wanted to warm up his body with my entire being. I wished to turn my love for him into an instant remedy, to bring back color to his face and sensation to his numb limbs. Just as he reciprocated my embrace, though, something puzzling happened: I sensed on my shoulder the faint noise of a newspaper being crumpled. Yet, I was aware that all the newsstands along the way were still closed at that hour of dawn.

I led him into the Workshop. The moisture infiltrated during the Christmas break had exacerbated the effects of the frost outside, making it even more bitter within than without. I immediately turned on the light of the main room and went to start the boiler in the closet next to the toilet. On my way back, I found him where I had left him: he was standing next to the counter, on which he had laid the newspaper. His labored breathing was condensing in front of his face, and he was looking around vacantly. Anyone observing him would say he was admiring the bizarre transformation of a mechanical workshop into a school of theater. But I knew he was focused on something else.

"Mom is fine," he said, turning to me.

I grasped what he meant. He thought that I would interpret his visit as bearing bad news. At that point, though, I already knew that my mother was fine. I wasn't shivering out of cold, now. I was scared of what he was about to show me.

NINE

Rome, present day

It's 10.50 p.m. on a Friday, and my subway train home is more crowded than usual.

Trusting in the laziness of the masses, who always tend to congregate in the central section, I'd hopped into the last carriage. Nevertheless, I now realize that there are at least two dozen people around me, counting both seated and standing passengers. As for now, things are within my tolerance threshold, but I must be careful not to overstep the mark. If I happen upon a station packed with commuters, they might get on board by the hundreds, all of a sudden. And I'd wake up lying in an ambulance with an oxygen mask on my face.

I'm mindful enough to regularly check the city news, keeping an eye open for dates and times of football matches, conventions, fairs, and other events. However, regardless of how vigilant I am, a sudden breakdown in the subway system, or a crowd of tourists who have lost their way, is enough for a throng of passengers to overwhelm me with their unbearable baggage of events, memories, and emotions. Once, when I was just one stop away from the station of Rebibbia, my usual destination, I found myself surrounded by a group of football fans who had no reason to be there. One of them wanted me to yell aloud something like *you thief of a referee*. Before losing my senses, I managed to remind him of his theft the previous day: a jar of mustard he had stuck in his vest while walking around a grocery store at Termini Station. He stared at me with terror and then darted away into the crowd. An instant later, all became dark.

Wait. Just wait a moment.

I know what you're thinking.

You have just thought that if you were in my shoes, *gifted* with the faculty of getting into other people's minds, you'd chase other goals than unmasking small-time thieves. I couldn't agree more. If I were in your shoes, I would also pursue quite another kind of satisfaction. My first choice would be to live a life of my own, without others always in my way. Free, once and for all, from what is going through other people's minds.

Let me work through an example to help you understand.

Imagine that you're a castaway on a desert island. You are completely alone, but you lack nothing: you have fresh water, food in abundance, a mild climate. You have even found a comfortable cave to shelter for the night. It's a dry place, cozy and free of annoying bugs. Of course, you'll feel deprived of all your things, but above all you'll miss the company of others, starting with those you care about the most: your partner, your closest relatives, your friends, your acquaintances. In short, you'll miss the people—their existences and your social life. Right from the moment you are shipwrecked on the island, every night, you have a nightmare in which someone you love dies. This happens for different reasons and in different circumstances. One night you dream that a friend is killed in an accident, another time an acquaintance dies from a disease, then it's your spouse's turn, then other relatives pass away. One by one, all of them kick the bucket. These nightmares are so real, so authentic and convincing, that every morning you wake up heartbroken, thinking these events to be genuine: these people have died. Disappeared forever. After a certain number of nights, you'll have exhausted each of your loved ones and you'll wake up in despair, wondering whether you are now indeed completely alone in the world.

That same morning, while scanning the horizon, you spot a cargo ship cruising offshore. You know that all you have to do is light a bonfire for the crew to see you. Just do that and they'll come and bring you back to the civilized world. At this point, I'm giving you two possible scenarios: in the first one, you keep hope that your dreams were nothing more than nightmares. In other words, you don't know whether those people have really died or not. You'll find that they are all dead only once you have been saved and brought back home. In the second scenario, instead, you know for sure that your nightmares were real: there is no one left, all your loved ones have indeed passed away. Now, if I ask you which of the two situations you'd favor, I bet you'd say the first one.

Congratulations, you've just chosen to live your life. Because the second scenario represents mine. In the first case, you'll go to collect the wood to light the bonfire for the crew to come and rescue you. In my case, I'll just remain seated, motionless, and let the ship disappear into the distance. When it comes to others, I have nothing left with which to delude myself. Whether their crimes are serious or petty, whether they have indeed committed their deeds, or just fantasized about them, they are always exposed before my senses. It's as if a continuous, appalling scream was yelling into my ears, without respite, what we human beings really are (I said *we* because, make no mistake, I don't exclude myself). That's why, from my perspective, everyone is already dead. Not by accident or disease. They died from lies, treacheries, meanness, and hypocrisies. For this reason, rather than lighting a bonfire to call for help, I would remain on my desert island, and allow myself to die.

Coming back to the present, I notice that on the train no one is talking to anyone else, except by text. Very few passengers have given up technology or keep it in their pockets. In the whole carriage, I can spot just a couple of books and the gnarled hands of an old man holding a newspaper. There's also an Asian woman, more or less my age. Head down, she is knitting with feverish ability. Meanwhile, I've found a free seat, and that means a lot to me. I put on my earphones and start Symphony

#2 by Brahms. I close my eyes and assign to my mind the task of visualizing each note, instrument by instrument, as to isolate the horn and distinguish the tones of the flutes. At the same time, I imagine invisible fingers gently gliding along the keys of the piano. These are my poor and cheap expedients to beguile my curse. But I know there's little that I can do. I know that my illness is much smarter, stronger and stubborn than all my silly tricks.

At the next station, the Asian woman stops knitting and lifts her work to eye level, as if to contemplate her feat. She seems happy with it. She's from Bangalore, her name is Ayn, and she's sixty-one. She will soon become a grandmother. In a way, we're colleagues: she works as a housekeeper in various Indian restaurants across Rome. As she seems to be a nice person, I wish I could stop it here and learn nothing more about her. I then decide to go back to my music, trying to focus on it with all my senses. Do you remember what you used to do, as a child, to avoid hearing, or seeing, unpleasant things? Do you remember the trick? You plugged your ears with your fingers, screwed up your eyes, and made weird noises with your mouth. There it is. To defend myself from the intrusiveness of others, I try something like that, asking Brahms for help. Unfortunately, it just doesn't work as well.

SECOND

Understanding

TEN

January 9, 1978 – Morning

I often think back to my father's visit to the Workshop, on that freezing dawn in January, and each time I see myself retracing my fateful steps towards self-destruction. So many events occurred that day, and so inept was I in coping with them, that I would be left scarred forever. The most disquieting of all—at least from my naïve perspective back then—was that I had lost along the way another fragment of my beauty. It seemed to be just another small sign of decline, hardly noticeable, but the cumulative effect was like adding successive layers of translucent veils. One after another, a single veil is added, each as fine as the other, but finally obscuring transparency. And the beautiful object beneath is suddenly eclipsed.

The people who used to gape at my beauty, like my father, were now disconcerted by how it was fading. And in such a short time. Not over decades, nor even years: in just a few months, a handful of weeks. On this particular occasion, though, it wasn't a mirror that had told me the bad news. I had read it in my father's gaze and, then, even more clearly, in his thoughts.

That morning, after entering the Workshop, I left him alone in the room for a few seconds. While he was silently looking around, I went to fire up the heating. Every fiber of my being, and no doubt of his, was imploring for warmth. More importantly, I thought it wise to impose a short delay between his arrival and what he wanted to tell me. I already knew he was there for the very same reason my mother had invited me for dinner, with such urgency, the night before. When I returned to him, a sudden thrill of fear wiped out the cold. He was standing before me, contemplating me in silence. For a moment, his figure, his entire body, transmuted into a mass of iridescent colors, with shades I had never seen before and to which I could not give a name. Each of them, however, had for me a clear meaning. They were neither letters, nor words, nor sentences: they were just colors. But they were colors that I could understand. I knew what they signified, both individually and collectively. I felt not unlike a musician who can mentally turn a chord from a score into its living sound. Or a mathematician who displays in their head the graph of a complex function just by looking at it. In a heartbeat, all my father's thoughts had pervaded my body. And this was his first one:

Vicky, my love, what's going on?

My looks were withering, and he couldn't explain why.

In an instant, the halo of colors returned to be matter, and then redesigned a body, and finally a face with the likeness of my father. It lasted no time, less than a second, but whatever he had had in his mind was now in mine too. If it were up to me, he could have left immediately. I already knew why he had come. In that moment, all my fears had vanished, and it seemed to me that what had just happened was quite natural. I felt just as if I had breathed more deeply than usual. My father, instead, was staring at me in distress, struggling to recognize me. In his mind, he was questioning my state of health. Was I sick? Then, what kind of disease could it be? He was wondering whether it could be something serious, or whether I was doing drugs. At that point, though, I stopped caring about his thoughts, my health, or anything else. The calmness of exhaustion stole over me, and I just wanted him to show me what he was supposed to show me, which I already knew, and then to leave me alone.

His arms stiff at his sides, he hadn't yet uttered a word. He threw a glance at the newspaper he had brought with him, which was now lying folded on the counter. I grabbed it myself and handed it to him with a gesture that meant: *Come on, be brave: I'm ready*. Helping him to the stool where I used to sit at work, I waited for his words.

"Vicky… you won't like what I'm going to tell you…," he said, laying his palm on the newspaper.

I remained silent. He was my father, and, from respect, I ought to have made things easier, but I decided not to cooperate. Antonello was everything to me, and no one could make me question him. Not even my father. Not even the fact that Antonello had been his mother's tormentor.

"Vicky… do you know that Antonello was jailed two years ago for beating his mother?"

I glanced sideways, downwards. A flyer promoting the school was lying on the floor. I bent down to pick it up, to avoid my father's gaze. *Intermediate Course in Acting*, the headline ran. I lay the flyer on the counter, taking care to turn it face down. I was just about to lie to my father, and the last thing I wanted was for him to realize it.

"Sure, Dad, I know he's been in prison."

Meanwhile, I was mentally rehearsing my offensive line. I had to go ahead with it all the way down, without ever yielding to my father's pressure.

"I wonder how you came to know it, though," I insisted, with an inquisitorial tone.

"Mom and I have hired a detective…well, *I* hired a detective. Mom has nothing to do with this."

I stood silent, staring into his eyes. I thought that my steady gaze was enough to express my disappointment at his recourse to duplicity. Without a word, he opened the newspaper and turned it towards me. The two yellowed pages of *Il Resto del Carlino*, Bologna's newspaper, showed more photos than text. But in no time Antonello's picture jumped out at me. Standing out from the criminal news section was the same photo that I had seen in his identity card. His wide-eyed look reached my eyes like a flashlight in the dark.

"Dad, I know that he has beaten his mother, I'm aware of that," I said. With a sigh of tolerance, I took the paper from his hands, then I folded it abruptly and put it back on the counter. The half-truth that I had just uttered was, in reality, blatant deception. I knew nothing, except what I had envisioned during that night's hallucination. My reply, though, seemed to imply that Antonello had told me himself, thus suggesting that he had regretted it. But I knew that this wasn't the case. There had been neither admission nor repentance from him. Nor did he ever mention that his mother had been hospitalized.

My father continued as if I had said nothing.

"Vicky, this man has harmed his mother and, she was hospitalized for three months because of it. What can you expect from someone who beats his mother half to death?"

"It was a terrible mistake, Dad, you can't imagine how regretful he is. And, anyway, Antonello adores me. He would never do anything of the sort to me, if that's what you fear," I answered, covering my lie with a dismissive gesture, to flaunt my absolute conviction.

"Oh right, he adores you. So, Antonello has beaten his mother because he doesn't love her, is that what you mean? You are saying that lack of affection for his mother, which I won't even attempt to deny, justifies him raising his hand to her? Is that it?"

I lowered my gaze for an instant, and he took it as a sign that he could continue to speak.

"Yet, there must have been a time when he had loved his mother, right? Then, for some reason, he stopped loving her, and here is the result. And what if one day he stops adoring you?"

"It will never happen. Ever!" I yelled out, without hesitation.

I wanted him gone. I needed to be alone. Right now. Alone, with no other thought but to clean the whole place. And the toilet as well. Perhaps with my tears. But alone, at least.

I told my father that I was sorry, but I wanted to be on my own. Try as I might to find the kindest words, all those I uttered acted as a strong thrust beyond the threshold. As I opened the door to help him out, a faint flare of winter sunrise tried to make its way into the room, but I immediately kicked it out like an unwanted guest. I slammed the door and locked the deadbolt in one movement. Then I went to the toilet and looked at myself in the mirror, frightened to find what I feared the most. And, sadly, I found it. I slightly twisted my body, then I lowered my head towards the toilet bowl and hit the target. At least I wouldn't have to clean up my own vomit.

ELEVEN

Rome, present day

Tijuana. I should have been born in Tijuana, Mexico, or in São Paulo do Brasil. Even Nigeria's capital—Lagos—would've suited me just fine. Just look at the homicide rates across the world and you'll find plenty of places where bumping into a murderer is almost as easy as setting foot outside. Now, let's not get bogged down with statistics, but just know that Rome, numerically speaking, is all in all a quiet place. It is true that there is—rightly—a lot of attention on femicides here. But the number of men who take out their wives and girlfriends is, by and large, small. This has nothing to do with my case, anyhow. I want to recruit a murderer from the street, not to raise one at home. You think me cynical? Well, perhaps you're right. You try to live a life like mine for a few decades and then we'll talk. In any case, if I don't conceal my cynicism, it's not just because I despise all forms of hypocrisy. That's just one of the reasons. But it's also unfair that I know your weaknesses without your being aware of mine.

Now, at a quarter-past eleven on Friday night, I have just left the Rebibbia underground station. From here to where I live, in the direction of Ponte Mammolo, it's about half a mile. It's a short stretch of road where—in a single night—you might bump into more drug dealers, thieves, scammers, fences, pimps, rapists (and even some murderers) than in an entire prison wing. Name a crime, and you bet it's well represented in this neck of the woods. Yet, it's almost ten years that I have been walking alone along this road, often late at night, but no one has ever laid a finger upon me. It happens, sometimes, that a kerb-crawler starts to follow me. He slows down to a snail's pace and sticks to me for a while, studying my figure and trying to guess my age, but then, as soon as I walk under a streetlight, he speeds up and disappears into the night. Speaking of which, let me reveal another thing about me. After extolling at length the beauty of my youth, now, with equal honesty, I want you to understand how exceedingly unattractive I have become. Vittoria Armieri, this wizened sixty-five-year-old toilet cleaner at the Ministry, is an ugly woman. I'm not sure that a detailed description of my looks would be helpful. Even a photo of me, with full evidence of my decay, could never do it justice. You'd still miss the immense gap between the young goddess of yesteryear and this crumpled old bag of today. It'd be unfair to put all the blame on the years that have passed, however. Time is cruel, but it's generally sincere. Satisfied with its own unstoppable nature, it needn't play petty tricks to wreak its deadly plan. True: the years, in their course, commit a series of assaults on our persons. From the disturbing onset of our first wrinkle to our complete decay, their work is relentless and unkind. The passing years are not just the kidnappers of our beauty. They are the tormentors of our cells, the molesters of our physical strength, the inexorable instigators of weakness and disease. In fact, time can be blamed for a multitude of sins including its inexorable final act. But this is not my case. There's no plausible connection between the natural physical decline and the ordeal that I went through. Other forces, much more devious, have come into play at some point in my life. With merciless virulence, they began to attack my beauty when it was at its peak. They have sapped it by dint of progressive mutations of my looks: deformations of their sweet and gentle lines in favor of cheap, coarse, and vulgar features. Across my cheekbones, once luminous and smooth, an unnatural swelling has ballooned. At the level of the brows, my forehead has thickened to the point of protruding, while dark circles are those of an octogenarian. Finally, my chin, once so gently shaped to resemble Leonardo da Vinci's *Lady of the Ermine*, is nothing but an undecided butt of my face.

Here we are again.

I know what you are thinking: *no wonder that someone so tremendously ugly wishes to die.* But you're dead wrong. Indeed, it's quite the opposite: my ugliness is what keeps me alive. By acting as a social insulator, it makes my illness tolerable. People don't talk to me, which is exactly what I desire. When they come across me in the street, they turn away, and I can ask for nothing better. Rarely does a person sit next to me, and this is sublime. It can happen that someone, caught by bizarre fascination for ugliness, starts to stare at me, but I don't mind: their disgust seizes them with such tyranny as to suppress any other forms of human baseness (like envy), and then I almost enjoy it.

Now, however, I must take my leave because it's late at night and I've reached my place. The third floor of this building, behind those two windows with lowered shutters, is where sweet home lies. I'm sure you wouldn't call it *sweet* if you just could see it. There are no paintings, no carpets, no tapestries. Any object that is not indispensable to my life is unwelcome. Forget the idea of finding some embroidery, a decoration, or knick-knack of any kind. No concession to aesthetic enjoyment has been made. The home of someone who can see everything ends up being like that of a blind person. In my flat, there are no mirrors, and, to avoid seeing my image, I have applied sheets of paper to all the windowpanes. A ploy that is now redundant: unlike Narcissus, whenever I happen to see my reflection, I instinctively look the other way. In addition, after decades of toilet cleaning—with my eyes fixed upon the rag at all time—I always know how to dodge my likeness in the glass.

But I must go now. Thank you for following me all the way here, and sorry if I don't let you in. There's no reason for you to come to my house, especially on a Friday night. You call it *a weekend*, but to me it's what life should be like on any given day: locked inside, without a soul around (living or dead), and free from the tumultuous past and present of others. Under these circumstances, I can even pretend, at least to myself, to possess an existence of my own.

TWELVE

January 9, 1978 – Mid morning

After curtly dismissing my father from the Workshop, I spent a good half of that gloomy morning tidying up the whole place. Then, when my joints got sore, I attacked the paperwork. That was the toughest part: with my mind elsewhere, I had to struggle extra hard to stay focused on names, dates, addresses, and numbers. In the end, though, both activities helped me regain confidence. My gymnastics with broom and rag, although hardly aerobic, had brought into my body enough oxygen to replenish my mental lucidity. As for my office work, it chased away the bad thoughts that had been incubating in my mind since my father's visit. Once I had completed my tasks, I locked the door of the Workshop and left the building, starting towards the street. I had a clear plan about what to do. Or so I thought.

It was almost noon, the temperature had risen, the snow thawed, and I was briskly heading towards my chosen destination. Prior to that, though, I stopped at a bar for a cappuccino and a phone call. As I approached the telephone, I wondered what excuse I would make with a doctor friend with whom I hadn't talked for months. Using the fewest words possible, I would have to make amends for my sudden disappearance, and for omitting to wish him *Merry Christmas* (which is how, together with a small gift, I used to reward him for his constant professional availability). After this parade of niceties, I'd have requested an appointment at his clinic at the soonest opportunity, possibly that very same day. These preparations proved as thorough as unnecessary. All I got was his voice on the answering machine. Without even waiting for the fateful *beep*, I replaced the receiver.

While I was sipping my cappuccino, irked by this setback, I was reminded of Antonello's aggression towards his mother and his photo in the newspaper. In a flash, I discarded that thought. It definitely wasn't a priority. A fit of rage, however deplorable, can happen to anyone, and this episode had been nothing more than a moment of temporary insanity. I would not have questioned my trust in Antonello over such a trifle. That's right, *trifle* is precisely the word that went through my mind. Shallow as I was, I didn't grasp the severity of Antonello's violence towards his mother, nor that of the phenomena I was experiencing. These were all issues that I had in mind to sort out, but some other time, not now. The real urgency lay elsewhere; more precisely, it was focused on my looks. What was happening to my face? Why was I struggling to recognize myself in the mirror? It was no longer a matter of occasional swelling under the eyes. Now, two dark circles, albeit faint, had steadily settled in. My eyes appeared opaque, as if the surrounding world was no longer reflecting in them. Even my lips, which from puberty onwards had blossomed into a robust vermilion, had lost definition: both their shape and their color had flattened, making them barely visible. What upset me the most, however, was the contour of my brow. Altered by a palpable thickening, it was now slightly protruding. It's for all these reasons that I had come to think of Giuliano. He was the eldest and wisest of our group of friends. Not only that, he was our round-the-clock medic, always ready to come up with a diagnosis for our pathologies (real or imaginary), morning, noon, or night of any workday or holiday. I had only to warn him of my arrival, and he would always find a slot for me. But today he wasn't at his clinic. Probably he had gone to the hospital for his shift. Flustered, I suddenly thought that he might be away on one of his impromptu vacations. He was wont to disappear for a few days, every now and then, and nobody had the faintest idea of where he'd gone and with whom. At that moment, I got distracted by a man in his late thirties who walked into the bar for a coffee. I drew his eye. Nothing strange in that—anyone who saw me for the first time would call me gorgeous, and despite my recent deterioration, this was still the case. As soon as I averted my gaze, as I always did with strangers, I realized the change in my motive. For the first time in my life, I felt what it was like to be ugly: shying away from the insistent gaze of men not so much to prevent unwelcome advances but to avoid their censure.

I approached the telephone again, this time with the idea of ringing my mother. I knew that she would bring up Antonello, but I also thought that listening to her voice, however sorrowful or angry, would comfort my heart.

She broached her list of grievances with the painful attack of arthritis that was plaguing her, then she quickly shifted to the subject that I expected and feared.

"Vicky, Dad has told me about your encounter."

"Mom, how can you call that an encounter? Dad came over just to tell me what you both think about Antonello, and I am now fully aware of that," I said, in a single breath. I continued, "That was why you just had to see me at any cost yesterday, wasn't it? If you had just come out with it on the phone at once, you'd have spared Dad such an early visit."

"Vicky, did you know it? Did you know he had beaten up his mother?"

"I didn't call you to talk about this, Mom. Listen, please. I'm fine, I'm living a wonderful moment with Antonello, what more should I tell you?"

"Nothing. I just expect you to understand how worried we are."

That was my parents' old trick: bringing up their affection for me, to burden me with their discomfort.

"Mom, isn't it you who always says that no one should be judged all their life for a single mistake? Then, why does this not apply to Antonello too?"

My mother remained silent for a moment.

"Why don't you come home? Can't we talk face to face instead of talking over the phone?"

Instinctively, I turned towards the large mirror behind the bar counter. It was some six yards from me, too far away to see my face in detail. However, I instantly knew how to reply.

"Mom, *home*, to me, is where I live with Antonello. Anyway, I can't come over. I'm sorry, but I'm too busy these days."

"Vicky…"

"Tell me, Mom," I retorted, approaching my threshold of tolerance.

"Dad told me… that maybe you should see a doctor."

"He should see a doctor, too, Mom. I've never seen him in such bad shape"

"Have you asked yourself why?"

This time I did keep mute for a moment. Enough time for my mother to understand that she had hit the mark.

"However, yes, I am planning to make a doctor's appointment," I replied, regaining confidence, "and that's why I can't come over and meet you."

I felt relieved that, before ending our call, I had told her at least one truth.

I immediately tried to call Giuliano again, only to hear, once more, his reassuring and professional voice-message. I had no other numbers for him, nor did I know at what hospital he was working. I decided to go straight to his clinic and wait outside the door until he was back. Surely, he couldn't be on vacation—I couldn't be that unlucky. Before heading to Giuliano's clinic, though, I had another errand to run. And to me, it was the most urgent of all.

THIRTEEN

Rome, present day

A gloomy drizzly day like today is a godsend from my perspective. It's eleven o'clock on Monday morning, and I'm strolling along the desolate pathways of Villa Borghese park, enjoying the sound of my own footsteps on the gravel and the slight patter of the drops on my umbrella. These are the only signals I can perceive from the outside world at the moment. Around me, there is just vegetation—verdant life blessed with inner peace. I venerate its intellectual emptiness, the absence of awareness, its vital non-existence. No memories, no disturbances, no emotions. It has no faults to throw at me, neither do I perceive past violent traumas which startle me. I wish people's souls were as generous as these branches, as delicate as these flowers, as light as these leaves. Grass, trees, and plants are pure innocence to me. Even carnivorous plants, despite their disquieting name, are as gentle as the others. Once, in a greenhouse, I saw plenty of them, but their emotional reactivity was perfectly aligned with their vegetative state. That's what the vegetable kingdom represents for me—the magic of life without the turbulence of existence. Animals, though, are a different kettle of fish: I rarely catch their emotions but, even if I do, I cannot decipher them. I feel their unrest or their fierceness, but I don't go much further. They fear me, though. They stay away from me. No dog has ever approached me, either to attack me or to beg for caresses. And even cats, which I adore, stare at me for a few seconds and then run away as if they had seen a car approaching. Mosquitoes, even, bite me very seldom.

Now that you know that I'm ugly, afflicted by such an illness and feared by all the beasts, you might easily think of me as a witch. I cannot blame you, though. If as a child I had been asked to imagine a witch, I'd probably have described myself as I am today. So, not only was I born in the wrong place, but also in the wrong era. If I had lived during the time of the Inquisition, my longed-for death would've come without delay. The only difference—instead of in a crematorium, I'd have ended up amongst the flames still very much alive and kicking.

Meanwhile, I'm approaching the bench on which I was sitting last Friday. It's precisely there that I want to find rest, possibly sitting in the very same spot—at the end on the right. After wiping down the bench with a tissue, I settle myself, mentally complaining about the slightly wet seat. I then place my handbag on my knees, as I always do. This time, I will have to hold the umbrella, and this bothers me a bit, but it's still better than getting soaked. Anyway, yes, I'm a creature of habit, just like many old people. In my case, though, because of my illness, I'm probably more set in my ways than anyone else. If a certain place has given me a shred of peace, without overwhelming sensations, I try to claim it as my own. I go back to that spot and do the identical things, hoping to revive that same condition of non-pain. It's as if there were two invisible brackets, in that place, and I could place myself just in between them, to leave out of my life all the rest, starting with the afflictions of others. Obviously, it's rare that a place remains such a sanctuary for any length of time. I can find quiet for a few visits, then something new always occurs to force me to escape and never return. I take it that it's just a matter of probabilities: the damnations that people lug around outnumber people themselves: they are, in fact, infinite. And therefore they are everywhere. I can try to elude them for a while, but it's just a matter of time—when I least expect it, here they come, and I collide with them.

Meanwhile, I see two policemen on their bikes pass before me. I follow them with my gaze while they quietly pedal along. Apart from them, and now two women who are walking a dog in the distance, I'm completely alone. Since there is still a good half hour before I start work, I can close my eyes and relish this moment of joy. Breathing in the moist air, I try to expand this instant—a tiny fragment of time that may mean nothing to you but is a small eternity of peace to me. Meanwhile, the patter of rain, insistent accomplice of the surrounding quiet, is bringing me a gift: a few drops of sleep, sweet and fleeting oblivion towards my beloved nothing.

Then, everything happens in a moment: I hear footsteps on the gravel speeding up towards me. A shadow approaches fast, almost touching my face. Instinctively, I clutch my handbag tightly with my left hand and just before opening my eyes wide I feel a violent snatch. The first image that I grasp is of a man in jeans, his head covered by a green hood. He's running away, holding my handbag. I'm frozen, terrified, unable to move a finger, let alone scream. Still seated, feeling my knees tremble, my gaze follows the thief, who is already several yards ahead. What happened to my reckless craving for a murderer, if a two-bit pickpocket is enough for me to lose my nerve? While this untimely question starts ringing in my head, or perhaps just because of it, I feel the tears explode from my eyes. My umbrella falls to the ground and I hide my face in my hands. But from whom am I hiding? And why? There is no one around.

Yet, no. Someone has to be there. There is surely someone around because I hear a man's voice. He's calling and getting closer. He's not talking to me, though. Who would ever address me as *madam*?

"Madam… madam… here it is!"

While I keep crying, I take my hands from my face and find a man in his sixties approaching at a rapid pace. He's breathless, wears a dark coat and holds my bag in one hand. He's holding it the way men do when they want to make it clear that the object doesn't belong to them: he's gripping it by the opening, its handles dangling free.

"He has run away... but I managed to tear it off him," he puffs, out of breath. I recognize him almost instantly. This guy is Domenico Morgelli, the murderer who last Friday was sitting on the bench opposite mine, now empty, with a sandwich in his hands. As I take the bag from him, my mind goes back again to his crime. At the same time, his docile gaze brings me back to his present life of redeemed man, volunteer ambulance driver. My gut instinct is telling me to look into my bag and make sure that my purse is still there. But I give up. I think it may appear indelicate. In the scuffling with the thief, this man's coat has become stained with mud. And he's still panting. If the purse were no longer there, he would feel frustrated by the futility of his efforts.

"You'd better check, though," he says, breaking off to catch his breath. "He could have slipped it out before I threw him down." Feeling puzzled, I look over at him. Then I quickly go to fumble in the various compartments of the handbag. My purse is no longer here. When I raise my eyes, I see Morgelli's hopeful expression turning into disappointment.

"I'm sorry. The way he wriggled out, I figured out he was a quick one," he says, shaking his head. Then, without waiting for my reaction he adds:

"He was a little taller than me... say 5 foot 9, brown short hair, jeans, and a green vest. I know it's pointless... I'm just telling you... to report to the police, you know?"

"May I give them your name? For the report, I mean."

"Sure, madam. My name is Domenico Morgelli and I live in Via Ostiense, 335. Would you like me to write it down?"

Instead of paying attention to his address—which I already knew— I take mental note of his slight accent. There's just a tiny hint of it, and of a special kind, typical of those who, despite their humble origins, have completed their studies or are very well-read. Also, I have noticed that expression of his: *I live in Via Ostiense*, instead of *I live at Via Ostiense*, as we usually say here—an affectation, probably unwitting, which attests to his having come up in the world.

"No, don't worry. I'll remember that," I reply, keen to end the conversation quickly.

My gaze follows him as he sets out along the pathway. While he cleans up his coat sleeve with heavy blows of his hand, I wonder at the idea that just because of an unfortunate incident like this, someone could show kindness towards me.

"I'm sorry about your coat," I tell him out loud, while he's heading away.

"No problem, madam. I'll be wearing my uniform for my ambulance shift now. Tonight, when I put my coat back on, it'll be okay," he replies.

While I'm still observing him, he turns for the last time to me. He lifts his arm in a gesture of farewell and, with a saddened smile, utters a last remark.

"You see, madam? Solitude is great, but it's got its flaws— sometimes it leaves you all alone."

FOURTEEN

January 9, 1978 – Late morning

I was twenty-two at the time. But I must admit that when it came to a sense of responsibility, I was barely a teenager. You'll see it yourself following my actions of that morning, when, after that phone call with my mother, I left the bar to head for Giuliano's clinic.

As I said, in the whirl of the recent events, namely Antonello's act of violence towards his mother, the veracity of my hallucination, and the loss of my beauty, I worried only about the last. That's where the real source of my anguish nestled. Unlike my other concerns, which I regarded as a secondary issue and a figment of my imagination respectively, I saw my increasing ugliness as a concrete fact. It was a truth that every mirror blurted out. Even though I had already discarded, as nonsense, the idea of serious illness, I wanted Giuliano to see me as soon as possible. Prior to that, though, I had another pressing issue to sort out. So, after leaving the bar, I hastened towards the main shopping street of the Flaminio area. There, I slipped directly into a cosmetics store that I had visited some months earlier. A zealous saleswoman, just a little my senior, listened patiently to my lengthy list of facial flaws. She hinted about a possible link with my menstrual cycle, but then, at my insistence, recommended an exfoliating gel and a set of creams. Just to be safe, I decided to buy also a light foundation, a revitalizing lip gloss, and mascara. Not only did I purchase this stuff with the feverish anxiety of a junkie from a pusher but, with an equal sense of urgency, I requested access to the bathroom for immediate use.

After twenty minutes of compulsive application, I left the store feeling reborn. In fact, I was confident that I had found myself again. While the sun was now warming up the late morning, I calmly strolled to Giuliano's clinic.

Along the way, when I came across guys of my age or a little older, I pretended to look elsewhere; then, on a sudden impulse, I turned my gaze towards them to check their reactions. Were they showing indifference to my looks? Or were they as sex-hungry as usual? Comforted by a succession of lustful glances, I arrived at Giuliano's medical office, a residential building in the Prati area. I felt great, happy, and confident. I contemplated for a few moments the main door, wondering why I was there, and whether I should go home instead, in time to have lunch with Antonello. Finally, I decided to enter. After a few words with the porter, I found out that Dr. Zeri—that is, Giuliano—would be back in the clinic at one-thirty, which meant waiting a little over an hour. Now that I was there, I thought it wise to stay. I had plenty of time for a quick sandwich at the nearby bar and—why not?—for a phone call to Antonello. Then, I could be back in good time to be seen as the first patient.

After a mediocre tuna *tramezzino* and an orange juice, I decided to ring Antonello. I expected, as usual, a terse interchange. I knew that he, deprived of the gestural eloquence and the expressive charisma he boasted in person, would reply in monosyllables. In fact, we had a one-way conversation. I told him that I had scrubbed the workshop clean and mentioned that I was about to see a doctor—*for women's stuff*, as we used to say at the time. Finally, after calling him *amor mio*, my way of releasing him from any obligation to reciprocate, I told him that I would be back by early afternoon.

An hour later, when Giuliano came into the waiting room, I was sitting opposite the door, between two elderly women and in front of a mother with a little boy. While greeting his patients with a smile, Giuliano immediately focused his attention on my face, but without recognizing me. He frowned at me as if in desperate search of a long-lost memory. And I felt awful.

"Doctor Zeri, good morning… I'm the first in line," I said, hoping that he recognized my voice and appreciated my playful intent in calling him *doctor Zeri* instead of *Giuliano*.

"Hello, Vicky," he immediately responded, surprised with pleasure and treating me with a casual familiarity in front of the other patients. "Just enough time to put on my white coat and then I'll let you in."

After closing the door behind us, Giuliano dispensed to me, with a simple remark, a pill of instantaneous efficacy.

"Vicky, congratulations… I see that love is good for you! I almost didn't recognize you."

That was all I needed. I could have left instantly, skipping all his meticulous questioning about which of my organs were ailing me and which weren't, or about my hours of sleep, my diet, the regularity of my periods and bowel movements, the color of my stool and urine. Whatever disease I thought I might have, I felt completely recovered already. Just to justify my visit, though, I hinted at the thickening of my brows, getting in return a puzzled look.

Giuliano measured my blood pressure, listened to my chest and then took out his prescription pad, on which he started to scribble down a list of examinations, including an X-ray of my nasal sinuses. While watching his pen flow and listening to his voice spell out one by one the various tests, I felt a mixture of pity and a sense of guilt. I knew I wouldn't have any of those tests done. I could already see that sheet of paper in the back of our knick-knack drawer, wrinkled and yellowed by weeks and weeks of our furious rummaging in search of bunches of keys, sunglasses, coins, and clips. I was young, beautiful, and I felt great. I had no disease whatsoever.

Just as I was about to leave, Giuliano asked me about Antonello, whom he had met just a couple of times while hanging around with my group of friends.

"Come on, Giuliano, I know that you're not all that fond of Antonello," I said with a smile, to play down something that had in reality hurt me. All my friends had rejected him, branding him as an arrogant and boastful dude. As I saw in him instead the absolute, a hero consecrated to myth, I had drifted away from them all, dumping them like a bunch of fresh flowers into a dustbin.

"Vicky, which fiancée of yours could I ever like?" he quipped, with his hand already on the doorknob.

Once in the street, I checked my watch and felt filled with joy. It was two-fifteen. By three o'clock, I would be back home to relish with Antonello our last carefree afternoon before the reopening of the school after the festivities. As I started quickly for the bus stop, little did I know that my happiness was just as ephemeral as the mascara on my eyes. Both would soon be gone, washed away by a torrent of tears.

FIFTEEN

Rome, present day

I must admit that I have been inaccurate in one detail. While it's true that I'm not used to being called *madam*, there's at least one place where they address me as *Madam Armieri*. That's at my bank—the very place I'm entering right now. I can't say that it's a widespread habit around here. Only the personnel who have access to my account call me that. To be completely honest, a policeman also called me *madam* recently—the young officer to whom I reported the theft. But that was not out of kindness. His complete sentence, in reply to a colleague who was handing him a document, had been: *wait, just let me finish with Madam… sorry what's your name?* Quite different from calling me *Madam Armieri*. In fact, before leaving, as he was confirming my personal information, he omitted it altogether. *You are Armieri Vittoria, right?* That's how he spoke to me.

Here at the bank, however, I am *Madam Armieri*. Certainly, I'm that for Cosimo, the financial consultant who has been working with me for almost thirty years.

"I'm really sorry about what happened, Madam Armieri. We have already cancelled your checkbook and your debit card. You were lucky that you had just thirty euros in your purse."

"And you call that little money? Thirty euros is a lot of cash. It was supposed to last until the end of the month! That's a whole ten days," I retort, crankily.

"Sure, Madam Armieri. I know how careful you are with your money," replies Cosimo, raising his arms in apology, "I just mean that it could've been worse."

"Of course it could have been worse: if they had mugged me last week, it'd have been a damn fifty. But, thirty euros is still quite a sum! Don't you think?"

"I do agree. I'm so sorry."

I look straight into Cosimo's eyes, as to advise him that I'm about to lose my temper.

I know that this guy is so honest that, in the case of a banking error, he would put down his own money to repay a customer. But I can't put aside the bad things that I know about him.

In response to my frowning gaze, I am met with Cosimo's expression of ill-disguised annoyance. I'm used to getting this kind of look from people. They think I'm just an old lunatic who loses the plot for no reason at all.

For no reason? Seriously?

Let me tell you a story.

People feel safe because they think their minds are impenetrable. Naturally they believe that their shameful secrets are inaccessible to others. And so, despite their guilty thoughts—mortal sins that they nurture in their minds—they carry on presenting themselves as paragons of virtue. I'll give you an example of their typical reasoning.

You don't know (how could you ever know?) that, deep down, I hope that my uncle's prostate cancer will grow fast so that I can cash in on my inheritance. And since you don't know that, what reason do you have to look at me with such disdain? Pay your respects to this pillar of society, you crazy old lady!

Here we go. With this example, I have let slip one of Cosimo's unspeakable desires. I didn't mean to, but I did it anyway. There are also other things, even worse than this, but I'd better keep schtum. In any case, let us make a distinction between his flaws as a human being and his skills as a consultant. Regarding the latter, I have no reason whatsoever to complain. Quite the opposite, in fact.

"How are my accounts doing?" I ask him.

I watch him shift his gaze to his computer screen. In a moment, he will ask me if I want to know the partial data or the total, as he does every time.

"Do you want to see just the partial data or…?"

"I want to know how much money I have stashed in this darn bank," I interrupt him.

"Oh, certainly, Madam Armieri. Here we go… you have nine hundred and thirty-five thousand, eight hundred and seventy-five euros and fifty-two cents. I can print it for you, if you wish," he replies, turning to me.

I shake my head and close my eyes. I remain silent both in reply to Cosimo's offer and out of irritation for what's going through his mind. Each time he reviews my balance, he wonders how on earth a toilet cleaner could have saved such a pot. The irony is, no one should know that better than him, since he's been looking after my savings for a third of a century. He's perfectly aware that it all started with a pretty sum inherited from my parents decades ago, to which I added the sweat of my own brow, with double shifts whenever possible and all expenses cut to the bone, if not to the marrow. Finally, to Cosimo's credit, I must add some thirty-seven years of good returns on my investments.

Come to think of it, though, I will never reach my goal of a million euros. I'm afraid I'll have to cut the reward to my murderer to nine hundred thousand. I know, this is all news to you, but this is the case—I'm going to leave to my killer all the money I possess (my entire assets except for my flat). Those are the instructions of my will, which I have entrusted to the law firm Massacesi, in a sealed envelope. Sometimes, I try to imagine the headlines in the news: LEAVES CLOSE TO A MILLION TO HER MURDERER. Anyhow, even though nine hundred thousand is not a million, it's still a tidy nest egg—well deserved compensation for the several years that my killer would have to serve in jail. I'm sure that I'd still have a sizeable queue of hopeful candidates willing to trade incarceration for it.

Yes, I know. You're thinking that I'm crazy. Well, let me tell you that your thoughts aren't original. Anyone would say the same thing. Your problem is the same as everyone else's—you make judgments without getting all the facts straight. Haven't I already told you to listen to my whole story before drawing silly conclusions?

In the meantime, Cosimo is looking at me is quizzically: he's wondering whether I have some sneaky plan about my investments, like finding another consultant. But I'm focusing on something quite different. I'm following my train of thought and I don't want him to stop it.

"Cosimo, I have changed my mind. Let me have my current situation printed; even the partial data, investment for investment," I say, in a commanding tone.

I watch him tapping for a few seconds at his keyboard, then, as he starts towards the printer, my mind goes back to the guy who retrieved my handbag yesterday, that Domenico Morgelli. No wonder he made that comment about solitude. Living in solitude is probably bliss after you've spent twenty-two years in jail, like he did. It's being alone once you're out of jail that must be unbearable. As for me, certainly, I do enjoy solitude. But is it indeed a pleasure, since I have no other choice? Isn't it like saying that you are happy on a diet when you really just have no food? Anyhow, that's not what I had in mind. What I was wondering is, why couldn't it just be him? I mean, why couldn't it be Domenico Morgelli, my murderer and heir? How handy such a booty would come in to a guy who can't even afford a dentist? It's true that he now drives an ambulance as a volunteer, which seems to disprove the saying, *once a criminal, always a criminal.* But he has killed two people already, and in my case he would be doing me a favor. Wouldn't it be great if this nice chap had a temporary relapse? Why not? As Cosimo comes back with the printouts and begins to display them on his desk, I find myself silently smiling at my silly thoughts: not only am I searching for a murderer, but since he would also be my sole heir, I want him to be hard up and of a sensitive nature.

How stupid of me. If among the downsides of getting old there is also the affliction of becoming so pathetic, then it's just one more reason to die soon. Finding an actual murderer, though, not trying to corrupt a reformed ambulance driver.

"Let's try to make up soon for the stolen money," I say, brusquely, in turning to Cosimo. Then I grab the printouts from his desk and stand up, poised to leave.

I'm moody and listless when I leave the bank to head off to my workplace. Today, I'm on the early afternoon shift, by far the most toxic. Toilets are always the first port of call for employees after lunch breaks. So, I'm going to have a lot more assholes than usual around, in both senses of the word.

SIXTEEN

January 9, 1978 – afternoon

When I came back home from the clinic that afternoon, I found Antonello exactly where I expected him to be—sitting on the couch with his legs stretched out on a chair and a book in his hands. That was his favorite position when he wanted to relax. Eager to join him on the sofa, I quickly slipped out of my puffer jacket and kicked off my shoes, sending them flying into the closet. All the while, I felt his gaze insist upon me, but as soon as I turned to him, I saw that he was absorbed in his reading as if nothing on earth could steal his attention, my arrival least of all. I went to curl up beside him, resting my head on his shoulder.

"Hello *amor mio*," I sweetly smiled at him, "life is tough without me, isn't it?"

"Tough enough… everything okay at the doctor's?"

"Everything is fine. I'm not going to leave you. Not in that sense, at least," I joked.

"Wow, how exciting. Which doctor did you go to?"

"I went to Giuliano's clinic. Do you remember him?"

"Giuliano?" asked Antonello, his gaze still glued to the book.

"Yes, he was in my group of friends. You've met him a couple of times."

Antonello looked up from his book, but only to stare ahead of him, as if he was struggling to focus on my words.

"Which Giuliano? That handsome dude with the glasses?" he said, contemptuously. "But he's not a gynecologist."

"Oh no, that's right. He's a general practitioner, he hasn't specialized yet because…"

"And what does he have to do with *women's stuff?*" he interrupted me.

I instantly realized my mistake: during my phone call, I had effectively used that expression. But that was just to avoid worrying him. Now the risk of misunderstanding was high. However, I thought I could still fix that.

"The fact is, before going to a specialist, I wanted to check with him, as he is a friend…"

Antonello turned to me. His inquisitive gaze, pointed straight at my face, revealed what question he had in mind from the moment he had seen me arrive.

"And since he's just a friend, why all that make-up?"

At this point, I hesitated. I remained silent. I couldn't think of any plausible reply without telling the truth. But to admit to him the decline of my beauty was unthinkable.

If you think you'll never forget your first kiss, just imagine your first slap. The moment I saw it commence, it was clear that it would be a backhanded blow, a bad one, destined to land between cheek and cheekbone. I didn't even try to protect myself with my arm, nor take evasive action. With passive resignation, I let the whole right side of my face—skin, muscle, nerves, bone, and cartilage—absorb the pain of the blow. The immediacy with which I burst into tears astounded me. I had hardly stood up, propelled by outrage and humiliation, when they were already pouring out, abruptly. It was as if, instead of being an emotional reaction, they were a mechanical and instantaneous consequence of the blow. Without a word, I fled and locked myself in the bedroom, feeling the weight of loneliness swoop down on me. I felt alone the way one must feel at the moment of death. I felt abandoned right when I needed all my loved ones right beside me: Mom, Dad, and my friends. Though I knew that I couldn't possibly find refuge in them. My parents, I had sidelined them, marking a sharp break between my old family and the new. As for my friendships, which had been strong until a few months ago, I had screwed them up big-time. I had sacrificed them all at the altar of my love for Antonello.

I remained in the same position for at least an hour: prone on the bed, biting my knuckles, as if by suffocating my tears I could stop the pain. But something different happened, the fatal consequence of my subjugated heart. Far from stopping my pain, as time passed, I became aware of its inexorable and dangerous metamorphosis. The physical suffering, which was brief, soon yielded to that of the soul. This latter, although unwilling to let go, slowly made way to a state of consternation. Meanwhile, rational elements were stealthily sneaking up on me. By breaking my emotional state, they started to instill the idea that I had my faults too. In the end, wasn't it me who had made the error of such heavy make-up? Antonello, unaware of the reasons, had probably taken it as a sign of my availability towards others: first of all, towards Giuliano, of whom he was utterly jealous. And Giuliano, on top of that, was one of my group of friends, the people who had snubbed and then rejected him. After working out the very good reasons for Antonello's fury, it took me nothing to begin to justify him, and, consequently, to acquit him. My logical process had culminated in a reversal of my initial state. After all, once again, wasn't this love? Antonello embodied love, right? So, every action of his ought to be an expression of love, even to strike me. Especially if propelled by a motive of jealousy. Even more so because justified by my own errors. After all—I came to think—what had been Antonello's slap, if not a caress armed with passion?

Meanwhile, as I wasn't hearing any noise from the other room, the mutation of my grief evolved into its final stage. It now turned into a growing concern. Overcome by the thought that Antonello had left me, I suddenly turned towards the door. Was he still furious? Had he stopped loving me? What if he had gone away, leaving me forever? In a spasm of panic, I rose from the bed to run and open the door wide.

But Antonello was there. He was in the same position as before: sitting on the couch, with his book in his hands and his legs stretched out on the chair. I let myself fall beside him, in search of his embrace. Antonello, unperturbed, passed his arm around my shoulders and started to caress my hair with his fingers. While I was trying to melt inside his body with every portion of mine, he kept stroking my head and reading his book. It was surreal. At that moment, I realized that I was lost, and that my being aware of it was to no avail at all.

SEVENTEEN

Rome, present day

At the beginning of the month, a colleague of mine fell ill. Since then, I have worked double shifts every day. This last week, especially, was very intense. It felt like one very long day, starting at dawn on Monday and ending on Friday evening—that is, this very moment. The display at the turnstiles, in fact, reads 22.02 when I leave the Ministry to head off to the metro station.

I like working overtime, but not so much for the cash on the side. The main reason is the joy of my journey back home, late at night: I'm so exhausted that, once on the metro, I slump on a seat and collapse unconscious. Those twenty minutes of nothingness—more or less the length of my journey—are the closest thing to death that I can happen to experience in life. A delicious appetizer, in the wait for the main course. In the catalepsy of that moment, I can rid myself of all human beings, together with whatever they have churning in their heads. Twenty minutes in which I set myself free from all their emotions, their sick fancies, and traumatic memories. As soon as I throw myself into a seat, my consciousness gets sucked into a black hole, often coinciding with entering the tunnel we meet soon after departure. Then, after a short but seemingly infinite sleep, I often reopen my eyes when I'm just a few stops from home, in a half-empty carriage which is rattling fast and shaky, while gusts of air mixed with noise filter from the open windows. Usually, at this point, I put on my earphones and abandon myself to Brahms' enveloping embrace. Exactly what I'm doing right now, while the doors open at the station of Pietralata, five stops from home. I tap the app of my phone and the music starts. Perhaps it starts too slow, but on the other hand, that's what Brahms is all about, and his Fourth Symphony, my dish of the day, is no exception. I notice that no passengers get off the train at Pietralata, and this irritates me. My dream of being the only passenger on board won't come true this time either. Instead, I see a young woman get on. She's in her twenties, dressed in black from head to toe, and settles two seats away from me, on my same side, just next to the exit.

Immediately, I feel something unusual.

As the train starts again, the girl places her backpack (which is also black) on the seat between us. I catch sight of a book and a phone in the side pocket of her backpack, but she doesn't take either. She closes her eyes and remains motionless—just the way I do (together with millions of other people) whenever I want to be alone with myself. It strikes me, though, that I perceive nothing of her. No thoughts, no colors, no strange signals. Nothing at all. It's as if she had no emotions, no recollections, not even a past life. A *tabula rasa*, a blank slate through and through. If I hadn't seen her enter the carriage with my eyes, I wouldn't even apprehend her presence. People like her, which—so far—I have happened to meet only twice before, I call *empty souls*. In both cases, I had remained stunned, without plausible explanation. Instinctively, I had thought of inventing an excuse to get to know those weirdos and pry a bit into their lives. But I immediately realized the absurdity of the idea. The one time that I find someone who doesn't burden my life with theirs, what do I do? I go and peek into it? Completely insane. My two cents, though, is that some severe traumas have shattered them, erasing their emotional lives.

Now, eager to free my mind from any intrusion, I divert my attention from this girl and the few other passengers. I close my eyes and go back to my music, waiting for the arrival of the first crescendo with the same trepidation of a patient who has just swallowed an analgesic and now expects an instantaneous effect. At the next station, no one boards the carriage, while half a dozen passengers get off, letting me savor a moment of blissful semi-solitude.

Halfway between the stations Ponte Mammolo and Rebibbia the train begins to slow down. Then, all of a sudden, it brakes twice in rapid succession, the second time more abruptly, until it violently screeches to a halt. The braking is so hard that it feels like the train has slammed into a wall, and I must hold on to the handrail with both hands and all my strength to avoid slipping off my seat and bump into the girl in black. The carriage lights flash three times in a row, and then they go off. While the music keeps playing in my ears, a wave of violence overwhelms my mind and body. My senses, suddenly disoriented, start sending me a barrage of messages which confusedly overlap one another. I see the color of a cry and feel the torment of a battered body, while the taste of blood fills my mouth and the smell of death my nostrils; then, annihilating Brahms's chords, a detonation implodes into my ears, as if the whole world had been sucked within my brains. With an infinite effort, I take off my earphones. In the pitch darkness of the carriage, I hear someone moan. One of the passengers, an old man, is crying out rambling words, while a woman's voice implores the lights to be turned on as soon as possible. But I already know that nothing serious has happened around me. This is not where the tragedy is occurring. Not on this carriage and not even onboard this train. It's far ahead, under the engine.

It's all dark around me. Yet everything is so clear.

I now feel another wave approaching, and this time it's made out of pain. I feel its mass getting closer, about to run over me. I shut my eyes tight and tense all my muscles to resist the blow that is coming. A wave of pain now passes through my body. It's the cry of a woman that has turned into matter. It's her pain, someone else's pain, but now it's becoming mine. It's so excruciating that it makes my heart vibrate: my heartbeats are tingling; my senses temporarily collapse into a void of consciousness, but only to come back soon after and hurt me even more.

It's happened before, it will pass this time too, I say to myself, to gain courage.

And indeed, it passes. Like other times, the wave washes by me, recedes, fades away.

It's over. I feel better now. It's just my heart that is still in distress, struggling to recover its rhythm. But it will make it. It always makes it.

"Somebody has jumped in front of the train," a voice beside me murmurs, suddenly.

In the dark, I turn towards those words, and immediately I understand that it is the girl in black, the *empty soul*, who has uttered them. She has spoken in a whisper, so that I only, among all passengers, can hear her. But there is another detail that I have caught, in her voice, and it makes me shiver: each and every one of her words is colored with suffering. It carries a strong and restrained pain. Why has she spoken with such a strangled voice? And how can she know that there's been a suicide? An absurd, unbelievable idea is taking shape in my head.

"She's a woman," I whisper in return, directing my voice, in the dark, towards the girl.

The moment the lights come back on in the carriage, the girl turns to me, and for the first time I see her face. Standing out of the pale and delicate lines of her visage, I meet her black eyes—black just like all the rest. And they are just as sorrowful as the words she utters.

"Yes," she says, "she was a girl of my age."

The idea that just a moment ago I had branded as an absurdity is now gaining ground. A concrete possibility has now struck me. But this time it's not coming in the form of a vision. It's a sudden awareness and, as unreal as it seems, it may indeed be true. This young woman dressed in black, this woman from whom I cannot grasp a single emotion, shares my same curse. I'm doomed, and nothing can change my tragedy. But, at least, I now know that I'm not alone in this world.

EIGHTEEN

January 10, 1978

The day after the incident of the slap, Antonello and I left home around noon, to get to the Workshop well in advance of the students. There's one thing that I vividly remember about that stroll—we walked the whole way holding hands. That was quite unusual, given Antonello's marked reluctance for behavior that he stigmatized as *schmaltziness*, especially if performed in public. That morning, I was walking on his right-hand side, my left hand grasping and occasionally stroking his knuckles. Only a few hours earlier, those same knuckles had hit me hard in the face, and now I was caressing them gently. Nothing can sum up better the countless contradictions that I embodied at the time.

Early that morning, the first to awaken, I had rushed to the bathroom to check my face in the mirror. Before I could even focus upon my now familiar alterations, hoping to find them fading, I was struck by something new and unsettling—damage that I immediately recognized as far more serious. A faint blood clot had spread just between my left eye and my cheekbone. It wasn't painful to the touch, but nevertheless sensitive. Out of despair, I instinctively closed my eyes as tightly as I could. If I didn't burst into tears, it was only out of fear that Antonello might hear me and wake up. I then looked back at my reflection, covering my right cheekbone with my hand. So desperate was I for a positive sign that keeping the bruise out of sight made me feel better at once. Examining the rest of my face,

I had the uplifting impression that my condition had somehow improved. The thickening over my eyebrow was still there, true, and my lips, as yet, far from their usual plumpness. However, it seemed to me that the overall picture was a better one. Thanks to this faint hint of self-confidence, I started to gently wash my face and then applied two thin layers of my creams, over which, eventually, I put a generous lick of foundation and a touch of blusher. That was when I noticed the utter irony—my make-up, the primary cause of the slap, had now become a ploy to conceal its effects. What I failed to realize, though, is that there had been no improvement at all. I was simply getting accustomed to my new features. In other words, my beauty continued to recede, but I had started to delude myself of the opposite.

During our stroll towards the Workshop, I came to think of the previous afternoon, when I had left my pillow of sorrow to rush out of the bedroom and join him on the sofa. His cuddles had soon turned into mutual rubbings of our bodies. Rather than by the quest for mutual pleasure, though, we were driven by conflicting self-serving goals. From my perspective, I wanted to redeem myself as soon as possible and return to feeling loved; as for Antonello, he aimed to reaffirm my submission, his tool simply switching from a heavy hand to an enlarged penis, impetuous and hasty in finding its way. It would be inaccurate to say that we made love. I would call our mating an appendage of the violence that I had suffered before. My participation, which might have seemed consensual, if not proactive, was nothing more than an unconditional capitulation. Through the concession of my body right after his slap, I had bestowed on him the sovereignty over my soul. I had officially signed my consent to a deal made of just one rule—he was my indisputable master. In fact, that very night, after a quick post-coital dinner, I had fallen asleep in his arms. Not unlike an abused puppy that pleads for its owner's forgiveness, I had remained in that position, motionless, for the whole night.

Nevertheless, while heading to the Workshop hand in hand with Antonello—I felt full of hope about our future. Despite his violence, I loved him even more than the day before. So, wasn't this proof that our relationship—regardless of events—was bound to grow stronger day by day?

During our walk, about halfway between our home and the Workshop, I turned to him.

"I talked to my mother on the phone, yesterday morning," I said. Then, fearing his indifference to this news, I went on, "I tried to calm her anxiety; you know how moms are, don't you?"

Antonello kept on walking, staring ahead of him for a few seconds.

"Anxiety about what?" he asked suddenly.

Antonello's ability in flooring me was only equal to my talent for getting myself into trouble. I had asked him that question to lure him into talking about his mother. I had hoped that it might be a way for getting closer. Perhaps, a first step for him to decide, one day, to share with me what had happened, or, who knows, to admit his repentance for his terrible deed. But now he had changed the subject, asking about my mom's anxiety. And, of course, I couldn't possibly tell him that she was nervous about our relationship, and about him in particular.

"She's got health problems," I managed to improvise, appealing to something factual. "After an operation on her knee three years ago, she started to suffer from arthritis. Some days, the pain drives her crazy."

"My mother suffers from arthritis as well," Antonello said, giving to the conversation the twist I had hoped for. I hence decided to keep him on this track—our concern for our respective mothers.

"I hope it's not as painful as for my mom," I said. "She's having ultrasound treatments, but sometimes even cortisone injections don't give her any relief. How is your mother being treated?"

"Same things as yours," he replied, apparently eager to close the conversation. Then, after a few steps, he added: "Nothing seems to work anymore, though. She can't even walk with her stick now."

She can't even walk with her stick now.

Antonello wasn't the type to ask many questions. Otherwise, he would have inquired about my being speechless. In the silence that followed, I felt compelled to recall my vision of that famous night—him raising a stick to beat an old lady. So far, I had always focused my attention on him and the elderly woman. Now, I tried to freeze the motion of that scene, switching my focus onto the stick that he was holding—precisely, on the shining silver knob of a walking stick. The emotional blueprint I had caught that night was to fully match with the unfolding facts. I could no longer tell myself that my vision had been sheer fantasy, or just a coincidence.

At that point, I should have gotten scared by the veracity of that night's vision. And I should have started to worry about these phenomena that were occurring to me. But I did neither. Instead, I was devastated at the idea that all of this might make me doubt Antonello. I saw my love for him jeopardized. But it lasted just an instant. I then held his hand more tightly and shrugged that thought away, as if it had been just a bad dream—one of the many that I had been having every night for months.

NINETEEN

Rome, present day

It's now two-twenty in the morning and I'm at home, in the kitchen. In front of the oven, I'm preparing an herbal tea for the two of us—for the girl in black and myself. In a minute, I'll be back in the living room, where we'll sip it together, staring at each other in disbelief. Then, still unsated of our talks but on the verge of collapsing, I'll make up a bed for her on the sofa, and we'll wish each other goodnight.

She is Nadine. And she's like me. She's pretty, and I'm hideous; she's in the prime of life, and I'm an old biddy; she's a genius, and I'm just a notch above a dimwit; she's a sweet *mademoiselle*, while I'm just a sour spinster. However, it's our common illness that makes us identical, or at least very similar.

Her full name is Nadine Mathieu, she's twenty-six and was born in Arles, to an Italian mother and a French father. She graduated in mathematics in Zurich, with the highest grades. Now, in less than two weeks' time, she will move to Pisa to begin her doctorate at the Normale University. All these things, I have learned directly from her, from her own lips. Not from strange visions, apparitions, or colorful suggestions. I came to know them thanks to the human words that she has spoken to me, and that I have listened to with my own ears.

She's like me, and I'm like her. Bizarrely enough, we feel like twins just because we are completely alien to one another. Each of us is an *empty soul* to the other. In short, we're both witches, but at least we feel normal when we are together. Right, normal. Only someone who recovers from a state of extreme physical disadvantage, such as a tetraplegic patient who learns to walk again, or a blind person who regains their sight, could indeed appreciate the joy we both are feeling now. Nadine says that she can't explain the reason for our blissful (and unfortunately temporary) communion. And if it's hard for her who is a scientist, just try to guess how hard it must be for a toilet cleaner. According to Nadine, our perceptions seem to emulate a principle of physics. They behave like water waves whose crests erase each other at the moment they meet. Overestimating my intelligence, she has tried to explain to me that something similar happens at subatomic level too, when light waves interfere with each other. I'll do my best to sum it up.

"It seems that we are the living representation of Young's experiment, where electrons are fired towards a screen through two nearby slits. When observed, electrons behave like particles; they pass through the two slits and hit the screen in a fashion which is predictable for corpuscular matter; if unobserved, on the other hand, they behave like waves: when they meet, they interfere: they can either overlap each other so as to strengthen themselves, or, in the case of destructive interference, cancel each other out. And this seems to be similar to our case," she said. Then, probably convinced that I had grasped her reasoning, she resumed talking. "But the difference is that Young's experiment is a mystery of physics, still unexplained. Our case, instead, is even more unfathomable, because there is no measurable phenomenon, susceptible to a physical explanation. We are just a mystery, and that's it."

While I pour some more hot tea into our cups, I think of this girl who is now sitting in front of me: an unknown person until a few hours ago, whom I'm getting to know from what she tells me, little by little. As I hand to Nadine her cup of tea, I get in return her look of gratitude, and I enjoy my ignorance of what's passing through her mind. Maybe she's thinking, quite rightly, that I'm a horrible old woman, and that living in a flat like mine, so bare and deprived of any embellishment, is an awful life. And perhaps in a moment she will be complimenting my turmeric herbal tea, refraining from expressing the disgust she's really feeling. The extraordinary fact, for me sublime, is that I don't know. I have no idea. Even though I may suspect that she's thinking all these things, and who knows what else, I can't possibly be sure of any of it.

I can finally appreciate the mystery that is concealed within a person. And I'm in no hurry whatsoever to unveil it. To me, Nadine is as inscrutable as a tree, or a flower, but unlike these, she has secrets to keep hidden from me, just as she may have a story to confide to me; and if she does that, it's because she wants to, not because of my ultra-nosy senses.

Right now, Nadine is savoring her herbal tea. She looks over the rim of her cup observing me as if I were an exotic bird. She, too, hasn't the faintest idea what I'm thinking, and she seems to enjoy this as much as I do. I might be doubting her whole story of an orphan girl who completed her studies with success. I might be wondering about her strange habit of dressing all in black; or about her backpack, which is too small for a girl who's moving to a new place; and yet, she can know nothing about my thoughts. She just carries on looking at me with equal sweetness. I cringe at the hideous scrunchie that gathers her hair into a ponytail, and I think how much better she'd look if she left it loose instead. Hundreds of people, before me, must have thought the same, and I can easily imagine her annoyance every time. Instead, she's now smiling at me. She might be guessing at my thoughts, but she cannot be sure that her surmises are true, and that's what matters to her.

I don't yet know whether our illness is identical or whether it's just similar. I hope that we'll find that out while getting to know one another better. But what I'm enjoying is that this will happen through words, sentences, ideas. Through the most natural process in human relationships, a pleasure usually denied to both of us.

After helping Nadine to the bathroom and passing her a towel through the semi-open door, I enter my room and sit on the edge of the bed. I consider the latest events of this night, and how the extreme improbability that they could have happened has been annihilated by their reality.

"Someone has jumped in front of the train." That's what Nadine had said after the violent braking.

Those words, which she had spoken with pain in the pitch black of the carriage, had reached me like a flash of light after decades of darkness. Next to me was an *empty soul*: a woman inscrutable to me who seemed to know what had just happened.

When the lights came back on, I finally met her eyes. Behind her gaze, shy and clear, like evanescent blue, there was an impenetrable fortress. She was just the face I saw and the words I heard her say, nothing more. A young woman dressed in black, with a black backpack. No iridescent mass had come out to reveal to me with gossipy malignancy what mysteries inhabited her mind, nor the backstory of her soul. It was just she and I. Just the two of us and my mere five senses. No sixth sense showed up out of the blue, poised to usurp the roles and contradict the judgments of its little brothers.

"Yes, she's a girl of my age," Nadine had said with regret.

"She knew she was sick," I replied. A few words, but enough to validate our mutual suspicions of being *equal*. Feeling guilty for exchanging coded signals in the face of a tragedy, we had started looking around with embarrassment. Meanwhile, the few other passengers, oblivious to the incident at the front of the train, snorted; someone was cursing the delays and frequent failures of the Rome subway.

The girl in black seemed to be lost in thought, then she raised her gaze towards me.

"What are the odds of us sitting next to each other in the same subway carriage?" she asked, perhaps with the intention of justifying the dialogue we just had had.

"I can't say; not high, I guess."

"Indeed, not high. Infinitesimal, I'd say."

She had remained for a few seconds in silence, as if she were performing a calculation in her mind.

"And anyway, we would never have spoken to each other without this accident," I added, indicating with my hand towards the locomotive.

"Yeah, I'm so sorry for that girl," she said, after a further pause. I had nodded at her words, deciding to keep to myself my ideas about suicide and death.

Meanwhile, the convoy had slowly resumed moving.

"There will be chaos at the station," Nadine had said, apparently concerned for both of us.

"It's possible that I'll faint," I said.

"I know what you mean," she agreed.

As the train approached the platform, the sounds of the tragedy were becoming more and more distinct—police and ambulance sirens, voices of the crowd huddled on the platform.

While we were both standing in front of the doors, which would open at any moment, Nadine had squeezed my forearm.

"Put your earphones on, keep the music high, and stand by me. Then, as soon as we get out of the carriage, just keep right next to me. Keep your eyes closed tight and focus on the music only."

Right now, back in the living room, Nadine is helping me to prepare her bed for the night, and she goes back to the extreme improbability of our meeting.

"What saddens me is that it took that girl's death for this to happen," she says. And, just because she has returned to this subject, I feel obligated to reply with all the frankness I can muster.

"I want to be honest with you, Nadine. I never feel sad for the people who have decided to die. Because that's what I want too."

THIRD

Reflecting

TWENTY

1978 – January to February

I could easily lay all the blame on Antonello for what happened that winter forty years ago. But I must resist this temptation. Faithful to the actual events, I must take responsibility for my mistakes, which were unfortunately grievous and countless.

I spent the weeks following the episode of the slap holding on to the fantasy that my life with Antonello, after a bump in the road (and on my cheek), was now sailing towards serene stability. I wasn't so naive as to imagine him kneeling at my feet with a wedding ring in his hand. But I was heartened by his frequent hints towards plans for the future, in which he always reserved a small part for me too. And that was enough to make my eyes shine. During my afternoons at the school, with Antonello's vigorous voice in the background, I often daydreamed of a home with just his surname upon the door (as was the custom of the time), and a bunch of happy bearers of that name within.

Speaking of more imminent events, though, a snag was looming shortly. In a matter of months, we would've had to return the flat to Antonello's friend, back from Brazil three weeks before schedule. Making projects together was therefore a must. Before long, we should have started looking for a new home, with our meager earnings soon burdened by this additional cost. Antonello, however, showed no signs of anxiety and, as for me, I regarded these problems as opportunities.

I nurtured the romantic idea that frugal meals on the table would feed a mutually selfless bond, just as a narrower bed would strengthen our embrace.

In hindsight, I now recognize that our quiet life of those days was just the effect of my new attitude—not yet entirely submissive, but increasingly docile and compliant. All the zeal that I devoted to Antonello was nothing more than a collection of the cares and attentions of which I deprived myself. Mortifying myself (and in a certain way my family too) was part and parcel of my insane idolization of him. Any personal issue that might crop up, like an urgent errand for my mother, I saw as an obstacle between me and Antonello—time, and love, that I was taking away from him. I considered a hindrance even my curse, which I didn't yet define that way, but which peeped out with increasing frequency. And so, instead of becoming aware of it, and trying to deal with it, what better expedient than ignoring it altogether? Why not sweep it under the carpet?

In the same way, I continued to pretend that nothing was happening in my looking glass, whereas, instead, I was losing my beauty day by day, albeit in barely perceptible degrees. My illusory panacea was to sleep a little more, change creams more often, choose my food with care. I was like a motorist who, unaware of the hole in the tank, thinks that keeping his foot light on the gas is all that it will take to make it to his destination.

Rarely did I think about Antonello's violence towards his mother. If it wasn't for my parents, so diligent in reminding me of it, I could easily have convinced myself that it had never even happened. So, here we go—I swept that under the carpet too. Likewise, I used to sweep under that carpet my last remaining shreds of pride, like those regarding my studies. I was only three exams away from my graduation, with a thesis subject already agreed with my professor of photography. Nevertheless, the only books that I used to open in those days were those that needed balancing at the Workshop. What I was failing to realize, though, is that all this garbage was coming from the same trash bag—my life. Then, a moment came when the heap of trash under the carpet was no longer negligible. It was so sizeable that I tripped over it and, finally, fell into it face-first.

By the end of January, Antonello had started a new class of beginners. Eighteen students had turned up, the largest group since the foundation of the school. Not only was it the largest, but also the most homogeneous: except for a thirty-two-year-old guy, an orthodontist, they were all twenty-something university students, many of them residents of the wealthy Parioli neighborhood. In addition to these affinities, they also shared a confused idea about the essence of theater. In short, they held that acting was fun but going to performances was dull. *Tread the boards but skip the stalls* seemed to be their motto.

Just two weeks into the course and these guys had already imbued the Workshop with their exuberant spirit. In front of a smug Antonello, their gags and jests had sneaked into Beckett's scripts, with colorful bursts of Romanesque vulgarity reviving, from time to time, the scant dialogues between Vladimir and Estragon. Looking at their rehearsals, you'd have said that the group of old actors led by Pistolesi had returned in disguise. Their grumbling voices had now been replaced by fresh and vibrant tones, and their clumsy postures, by athletic and lively gestures. Finally, instead of those frequent senior moments, a harbinger of confusedly stuttered lines, you now had impromptu and creative variations of the original scripts. The tendency to mess things up, though, was pretty much the same. The only true difference was that the old actors had seen the Workshop as a place of leisure, whereas for the group of young students it was the venue for their flippancy. Far from being keen learners, they were fans of their own amateurism. He who acted worse gained more laughs, thus becoming the hero of the hour.

One evening, on our way home after a lesson more unruly than usual, I dared to make a timid objection to Antonello.

"You let those guys get away with anything."

Why wasn't he as severe as he had been with Pistolesi's group? Why using double standards in the face of almost identical situations?

"I know what I'm doing," he replied. Then, still unsatisfied, he continued. "Anyway, who runs the place?"

Focusing on the similarities between Pistolesi's group and this new class, though, I had failed to grasp the decisive difference between them—the real reason that Antonello treated them differently. With the sole exception of Emilia, our earliest student, the old actors were all men. As for the young students, the majority were instead girls—pretty, well-educated and well-off gals. No wonder that Antonello had found in this new group not just a class but an audience—an actual public, largely female, all for himself. So, instead of a *bunch of old farts* from which to distance himself through authoritative manners, here he had a merry group with which to bond. And in fact, day by day, week by week, he became one of them. Just to be clear, he always stood a good notch above them. He was a chum, yes, but forever poised to prevail as the first among the peers. While he rarely got furious at them collectively, he used to scold them one at a time. And, coincidentally, it was never a girl. When Antonello had to pick on someone during class, it was always one of the guys. If he had to humiliate someone in front of the others, he unfailingly went for the cutest guy, the most polite and attractive. In other words—his direct rival. What more effective way to avert the deep-blue eyes of Marica, the sweetest gal of the group, from this chap? What better trick to draw them upon himself? To prevent Marica from devoting those sensual lips to that sap, nothing was better than having her hanging from his own.

Since these classes were on Fridays and ended around 9 p.m., we had started the habit of a pizza-night all together in a restaurant a few minutes' walk away. During those meals, I tried to be part of the group with all my might. My efforts, though, regularly crashed against the barrier, as much invisible as impenetrable, that separated the artists—that is, Antonello and the guys—from everyone else—that is, me. The main reason for my discomfort during those dinners (from which I wished to excuse myself from the moment I sat down) was that I felt excluded. But the progress of my illness also played its part. Its course was devious and made of discontinuous symptoms, and I was beginning to feel its weight, especially on those occasions. Sitting with that boisterous group was enough to mess me up. At that point, their faces would turn into a din, their voices became colors and their gestures—sensations. The reality around me started to lose sharpness. Each of my senses was shaken by that chaos, and a feeling of exhaustion pervaded me.

One night, in late February, I decided to skip the pizza-party with Antonello and the students. Complaining about being tired after some nights of sleep deprivation, I apologized to them and promised that I wouldn't miss the following Friday's date. Antonello, last out of the Workshop, I arranged to meet later at home.

When everyone was gone, I left the door ajar and breathed a sigh of relief—*blissful solitude*, I thought. My idea, at that moment, was to grab my bag, put on my puffer jacket, and walk straight home. Just before closing the door behind me, though, I changed my mind. I thought that it might make sense to stay and start the cleaning. Thus, I would spare myself the next day's early rise, indulging, instead, in Antonello's embrace. In no time, I made up my mind. Pulling on the rubber gloves, I grabbed my instruments of tranquility: the broom and a bucket full of water, complete with rags and detergents. Not even five minutes had passed when I heard some hesitant steps come near; at the same time, my eye fell on a floral backpack half-hidden by a chair. As soon as I saw Marica approaching and looking around as if in search of something, I took the backpack in my hands and went towards her. I stared at her eyes—two sparkles of sapphire. Two blue marbles that darted out from her patrician face: features of ancient Rome, passed down through generations of noble marriages.

"Here it is," I said, with a smile, moving a step towards her.

Just seconds earlier, upon hearing that someone was coming back into the Workshop, I had realized the risk: if one of the students had caught me with my hands in the bucket, the barrier that stood between them and myself would suddenly double in height and thickness. But there was something else, much more serious, that was about to happen. On one side there was I, with my yellow rubber gloves; on the other side, there was Marica, with her blue eyes, her ash-colored hair, and her diaphanous hands, tapered towards fire-red-enameled nails. Then, just between us, where our hands were about to meet, the floral backpack stood out. In that confused mishmash of colors, a shining fragment of information flashed into my mind. It said that along with that backpack, I was handing over to Marica Antonello too.

"Thank you," Marica said. And ran away.

TWENTY-ONE

Rome, present day

Nadine has been my guest for two days now. On the night that we met, she had just arrived from Zurich with the idea of spending two weeks in Rome as a cultural tourist and then move to Pisa for the start of her doctorate. That very night, she was supposed to stay at an Airbnb studio apartment in the Romanina area, about a mile from me. The accident in the subway, though, changed everything. We hadn't left the metro station yet, and we already knew that we couldn't possibly just wave goodbye and take our separate paths.

"I indeed wonder about the odds of such an encounter," she had said while crossing the road, her arm in mine. Then, without waiting for my reply, she had continued: "I always enjoy such computations, but in this case, I'm afraid I'll have to settle for a random number. Are you okay with a probability of one in twenty-four billion?"

"A good reason for keeping in touch," I had said, on the walk home.

So, yes, Nadine has been sleeping here for two nights—except that we are sleeping hardly at all. The first night, after sipping our herbal tea, we were about to go to bed, already exhausted, when I was suddenly reminded that I hadn't offered her any food. That's another peculiarity of living alone for decades: you get to thinking that your eccentric habits are normal. It was nearly three o'clock in the morning when it came to me that only an ascetic hermit like me can go to sleep on an empty stomach. While leading her towards the kitchen, I tried to recover a long-lost memory—the last time that I had enjoyed a meal with someone else. I failed, though.

Sitting at my kitchen table, that night, we struggled to keep our conversation on a single topic for more than a minute. Just like the food we were sharing, which I had cobbled together from my half-empty fridge, our conversation had been varied and fragmentary. We jumped from her studies in math to mine at the Academy of Fine Arts, from her temporary job as a hairdresser in Zurich to my humble position at the Ministry, with little hints, on her part, at the loss of both parents and to a love story she had recently ended. During that late-night-early-morning dinner, our respective *illnesses* had always remained on the sidelines. It was a subject that we knew we had to deal with sooner or later, but without too much haste to get there. Free from the lives of others, we were enjoying each other's company. A moment of unusual normality that I certainly didn't want to spoil with my troubles. And I thought she felt the same.

It was dawn when we finally decided to head for our beds.

The next day, Saturday, we woke at noon. We were silently having a coffee in the living room, when I realized that there was no need for me to make a formal invitation: we both assumed that she would stay at my home until her departure for Pisa.

"How come you dress all in black?" I had suddenly asked her, with an impertinence that I immediately regretted.

"It helps me unload my *flashes* when I feel them come," she replied. "To protect myself, I instinctively lower my gaze, and a colorless backdrop helps." While listening to her words, I quickly imagined myself in a black outfit from head to toe. As if being ugly and old, I thought to myself, wasn't enough. However, I was surprised, because I had never imagined that I could find relief just by dressing in this way.

Right now, two days after our encounter, it's a rainy Sunday afternoon, and Nadine has offered to cut my hair.

"Cut my hair? Why would you do that?" I asked her.

"I want to feel young again," she replied, closing her quip with a short, deep laugh, as she often does.

She's referring to her early Zurich years as a student. At the time, she had a temporary job at a hair salon. With that money, not only did she pay for her studies, but she could also afford a monthly trip to Arles, to visit her parents.

"It's close to forty years that no one has dared to touch my hair," I protested. In reality, it's even worse—I cut it myself a couple of times a year, with some random snips and without a mirror.

"That's exactly why it's time for proper treatment," she retorted, taking my hand and leading me to the bathroom.

Now, after placing a towel over my shoulders, she is providing me with more details about that *friseur salon* in the center of Zurich, mostly frequented by wealthy bankers' wives. She used to work there three afternoons a week and the whole day on Saturdays.

"No problem with all those women around you?" I ask her.

"Well, there wasn't much going on inside my clients' heads. Guess what—they cared more about the outside."

I dwell on this joke of hers: if a week ago someone had told me that one day I would smile again, I would have called them crazy. Meanwhile, she continues with her story.

"At that time my *flashes* were rare, and I had somehow learned to keep them under control. Or, at least, that's what I thought," she says.

She calls *flashes*—a word without negative connotations— what I call a *curse*. I wonder whether she has found a silver lining where I have always seen only clouds.

Now and then, she suspends her story to comment on the haircut she's about to embark upon.

"Of course, a mirror would help," she says while massaging my hair with her shampoo, its bottle all covered in German writing.

"No mirrors in my home. I'm aware enough of my ugliness and there's no need for new confirmations."

"I don't think you're ugly," she says.

"Be careful, Nadine. The fact that I can't perceive your lies doesn't mean that I must believe them," I replied, and we both burst out laughing.

With a quick snip of scissors, whose pleasant sound I had forgotten, she starts to cut my hair. She leans over to me, focusing on the cutting, then, at times, she interrupts her job and stands straight behind me. At that point, she places her fingertips on my head as if to check that everything is fine. Meanwhile, after a few more snips, she returns to telling me about her flashes and how she had noticed their onset at an early age.

"As a child, I felt on my skin the pain of others, and with an intensity that I now define as pathological. The bad mark of a classmate was enough for me to feel sick—much more seriously than if it had happened to myself. And it was not mere compassion. I felt a sadness grow inside my chest that made me lose both my sleep and appetite. If I heard of a kid whom I knew was being abused, I could weep for days. At other times, I remained in pain for weeks over a dead animal on the side of the road. An excess of sensitivity that I carried on throughout my adolescence, at first believing that it was normal, but gradually becoming convinced that something was wrong."

Out of the corner of my eye, I can observe my greyish locks land one after the other on the floor. In the meantime, I dwell in amazement on Nadine's lucidity in assessing those facts. I used to have similar feelings as a child, but I had never seen a connection between my inconsolable sorrow for the misfortunes of others and the curse that I carry to this day. My thoughts, however, don't divert my attention from Nadine's reconstruction of the events.

"I was sixteen years old when Juliette, my dearest friend, lost her father. As it had happened abruptly, in a work accident, it was no wonder that she went into a mild form of depression. In those same days, I developed my first signs of anorexia. In a way, my reaction had been more severe than hers. A few weeks later, a new episode occurred—a clear sign that my sensitivity was turning into something else. That morning I woke up with the vivid memory of a nightmare; it had to do with Juliette's dad. Before I even had breakfast, I wrote down every detail of that bad dream in a notebook that I kept hidden in the house; then I rushed to school. During a break between lessons, Juliette told me about her unsettling dream of the previous night. With goosebumps running down my spine, I listened to her account of her nightmare—identical in every detail to my own."

After completing the haircut, Nadine lays down the scissors and stands to face me. Peering into my face, she slightly tilts her head in admiration of her work. Then she passes her fingers through my wet hair, gently tapping them on my scalp. In the meantime, I dwell on her delicate visage and her glossy hair. I'm tempted to ask her whether, in conjunction with those phenomena, she had noticed a change in her looks, but I refrain from that, letting her continue her story.

"At the age of thirteen, my first flash occurred. An aunt of mine, my father's sister, had come to dinner with her husband. Even though he was just an in-law, I was very attached to him. He was a sweet man and always had a little present in his pocket for me. That evening, a moment before we sat down at the table, a flash of light crossed my mind. It was not an image, yet I could somehow see it: he was lifeless, lying on a hospital bed, his head bandaged. He died a month later, following a futile attempt to remove a brain tumor."

We remain silent for several seconds. Hard for me to say whether she's focused on my hair, or whether she's recalling those moments.

"We are well on our way," she says, changing her tone and the subject. "Now I'll give you a quick rinse, then try my own kind of styling. Just a couple of curlers to add some movement to the hair."

I'm so impatient to know more about her past that I'll put a good face even on such torture.

"Other incidents like this followed, more and more intense and closer together. Sometimes they involved events that had already occurred, sometimes things that would happen next; either way, a tragedy was looming in my world: if it wasn't a death, it was a disease, or an accident, or in any case a reason for sorrow. At that point, I decided to start to fight. I wanted these episodes out of my life. If I couldn't get rid of them, I had at least to contain them as much as possible. It was almost by chance, when I was in my senior year of high school, that I found refuge in mathematics. It happened one morning, while my teacher was explaining quadratic equations at the blackboard. At that moment, I felt a flash coming that in some way involved her. It was something bad; they're always bad, and I wanted to know nothing about this; I didn't want to see it. At that point, I decided to focus with all my might on the equation she had written, trying to solve it in my head. It was hard because it was a two-unknown equation, but I made such a tremendous effort to work it out that the flash started to recede, gradually, until it disappeared."

"What? You mean that you fight your flashes by making calculations?" I ask, hopeful of a foolproof cure.

"Unfortunately, it's not that simple. Over the years, the flashes became stronger and more frequent. I had to move on to more and more complex calculations to keep them at bay, and sometimes that didn't work either."

"I understand," I say, trying to conceal my disappointment, especially recalling how poor I was at mathematics.

"In any case, everything went on quite smoothly for a while," says Nadine, as she applies the first curler to my hair. "My early years in Zurich, especially, were great: with math problems always in my head and my job as a hairdresser, I was busier than ever, and I managed to keep my flashes at a distance."

Nadine walks in front of me to check my hair from this other perspective. Glancing at me for a moment, she shakes her head. I guess she's regretting the lack of a mirror. She then goes back to her working position and unrolls the curler, only to adjust it a few inches forward. Now she seems more content and picks up her story where she had left off.

"One afternoon, an incident occurred. It was the last Saturday before Christmas, and the salon was full of clients, all more demanding than usual. That made my boss and colleagues rather stressed—the worst thing that can ever happen around me. At that moment, I was busy with the tint of a woman in her forties; not one of the most frequent customers, but a familiar face in the salon. At some point, my boss called me aside and reproached me for my slowness. She was absolutely right, because, as a security measure, I had intensified my mental math, and this was slowing me down. After her scolding, though, it became hard for me to focus on numbers, then arduous, and eventually impossible. At that moment all the calculations faded out of my mind, carrying together numbers, symbols, and any mathematical notion that I possessed. Suddenly the flash kicked in. I sensed that it was about to arrive, but I failed to understand how powerful it was. There was nothing I could do by that point. In fact, I heard it. I kind of saw it. I felt it. *It's a girl, four or five years old, walking in the street with her mother. Suddenly, she escapes her mother's grip. A car comes and knocks her down.* I remained paralyzed for a moment. Then, when I looked up at the mirror to return to reality and resume my work, I noticed my client's tears: try as she might to dry them with her wrist, they kept coming copiously, overwhelmingly. At that moment I fainted and fell onto the floor. A few hours later a colleague of mine confirmed to me that two years before, just a few days before Christmas, that woman had lost her child in a car accident. When she told me how it occurred, I started weeping. I went back home and spent three days locked in my bedroom, crying all the time."

Once again, Nadine pauses to focus on my hair, or, more probably, to retrace that memory. As for me, hoping that she will resume spontaneously, I try to resist the temptation to encourage her to keep talking. After several seconds of silence, however, I decide to press her.

"You mean that focusing on the equations wasn't enough?" I ask.

"On that occasion, I realized that I couldn't hope to defeat the flashes just by doing equations. I had to start a relentless war. Mathematics could be a tool, no doubt, and the fact that it was my passion was certainly helpful, but if I really wanted to have my life back, freed from the lives of others, I had to do more."

"What do you mean by *more*, Nadine?"

"It's not easy. It's not easy at all, Vittoria," she replies, instantly dampening my hope.

The suspicion that she wants to hide something strikes me, and I don't scruple to point it out.

"Nadine, I can't believe it—you know of a way to hold my illness at bay and you are keeping it from me. Is that so?" I ask, trying to be honest without being rude.

"The thing is, Vittoria, that you're looking for the miracle pill—the trick that sorts out everything with just a gulp, as if by magic," says Nadine.

I keep quiet. Since Nadine herself waits a few seconds before resuming, my silence sounds even more like an admission.

"My secret, Vittoria, is fighting. And to do that, I deploy my army, with my soldiers, their weapons, their will to win. An army also made of numbers, of course, but propelled by my passion for them, and my will to see them triumph. But this is *my* army, and it took me years to recruit it. Have you ever really fought, Vittoria?"

Nadine completes her job with two touches of mousse, and I remain silent. I'm thinking about how I threw my life away. She has been able to discover a passion and, through it, fight her flashes. As for me, I stuck to a broom in the way I could have to a bottle. While she vigilantly suppressed any upsurge of her illness, I left the field open to it, feeding it with my self-pity. While Nadine armed herself with her will and went from difficult equations to more complex ones, as far as to insoluble problems, I found nothing better than crying for myself with a piece of classical music plugged into my ears.

Not only have I never fought my illness, but I have never even contemplated it.

Too late, time is up—I say to myself—while Nadine, behind me, turns on her portable hair dryer.

TWENTY-TWO
March 19, 1978 – Early morning

My father's death certificate reports the date of March 20, 1978, and that's correct. The time is no less precise: 21.17; nor the place where he died: the Gemini Hospital in Rome. The one item that is wrongly reported is the cause of death. It wasn't a heart attack that killed him. It was a bullet of a particular kind, devoid of both casing and gunpowder. It was a bullet that was completely intangible, but no less lethal. Antonello fired it, pulling the trigger of a gun that I myself was holding. Afterwards, as a further demonstration of our culpability, Antonello and I hastened away from the scene, taking separate paths. This wasn't done so much to escape the police, since there was no investigation into us, but rather to lose sight of each other.

That bullet took about eleven months to work its way to my father's heart—a trajectory just as long as my story with Antonello. This means that I had all the time necessary to warn him that the shot had been fired, to urge him to dodge it. In those eleven months, though, I failed to do any of this. What I did instead was lodge the butt of the gun more comfortably in the hollow of my hand. For the first phase of the bullet's path I can claim some justification. But I have no excuses, nor alibi, for the moment right before the impact, that is, in the last two days of my father's life. If I had released a cry of warning, even at the last moment, I would have saved him. As a result, my mother wouldn't have died a few months later, and I would have spared myself a life of despair.

It was late March, and for at least two weeks I was aware of the story between Antonello and Marica. Not only was I aware of their affair, but I saw it growing stronger right before my eyes. There was no need of paranormal faculties to realize that; an average female intuition, even one intoxicated by obtuse love, would have sufficed to make suspicions into certainties. It was evident that some of Antonello's daytime disappearances were of the same nature as his late-night returns. Our sex life, once so fulfilling, was now slipping away, and his absent-minded attitude, like a crossfade effect, becoming increasingly intense. The blindness of my passion, in alliance with the futility of my perceptions, had turned me into the perfect idiot, the ideal partner for any cheat.

This was my mood of all that period, and in particular March 18, when, at about 2 o'clock in the morning, Antonello came home. I was in bed, with the light off. Huddled in my grief, I felt a bland relief in hearing the front door close, followed by the rapid rustle of clothes dropping to the floor. I listened to his steps approaching the bed and finally felt his body, exhausted by causes familiar to me, collapse heavily on the opposite side of the mattress. There is no doubt that my tears of that night, however restrained, had reached Antonello's ears with equal clarity. But he gave no sign of it. His reaction was to annul the sound frequencies of my sobs with those of his own breathing, which soon became deep, and then turned into slight snoring.

The question you're asking yourself—how I could still love him—doesn't take into account my emotional state of the time. I know that what I'm about to tell you will leave you aghast. But I said from the beginning that I would keep nothing from you, revealing all the unedifying aspects too. In my life, I have scrutinized the feelings of too many people to deny you, now, the full sight of mine.

The thing is, I somehow justified him.

He was cheating on me, of course, but I had betrayed him, too. From the knockout I used to be when we had met, I was now freefalling towards becoming a barely pretty girl. I had introduced myself to him a goddess, but the figure I was now putting before him was increasingly commonplace and dull, transfigured by drudgery and sapped by his waning attentions. A ragazza in rubber gloves; a servant who occasionally happened to sit at the artists' table, with Antonello at its head.

That night, however, my tears didn't disturb Antonello's sleep. On the contrary, they perhaps even induced it. In fact, the next morning he awoke first to prepare breakfast. When I got up from bed, a few minutes later, I found him peering through the window of the kitchen with a steaming cup of coffee in his hand.

"Good morning," I said, trying to sound natural.

"Hello Vicky, did you sleep well?" he asked, turning to me.

I noticed that there was no sarcasm in his voice, nor desire to provoke my outrage. The opposite, in fact. Six hours after his fuck with Marica, he had now shifted his thoughts to the Workshop: that afternoon a new beginners' course was supposed to start, and everything had to be impeccable.

"Not really; actually, I'm not feeling well this morning; I was thinking of swinging by my mom's house," I replied.

"Of course, I understand," he said, approaching me with thoughtfulness. He stroked my head, gently, and after pulling me towards him, he started caressing my hairline with his fingertips. There was no erotic intent, but it was enough to bring me back to our passionate moments and to unleash in me a barrage of questions. *What if his affair with Marica is over? Is he perhaps regretting it? What if he has decided to come back?* We remained in that position for half a minute. While he was toying with my hair with his absent gaze directed towards the window, I stood there, motionless, fearful of disturbing his thoughts. My hope was that his tender caress would soon turn into an enveloping and liberating embrace. A real kiss and I would have forgotten everything. No need of his repentance, nor of my forgiveness; because there would be no longer any guilt to confess, nor any pardon to be granted. A real kiss, right at that moment, would've hit me like a benevolent shock, instantly wiping away all recent events, my doubts and his betrayal.

But no hugs followed. Antonello moved away from me and approached the stove to pour some coffee into his cup.

"Do you want some more?" he asked me, pointing to the coffee pot.

"No, thank you," I replied, swallowing the knot of sorrow that I felt swelling in my throat.

"Just spend the morning with your mother, Vittoria, and don't worry about the Workshop; nothing is going to happen if you take a day off," he said, in an obliging tone.

"And you? What are you going to do, then?"

"I must go to the library, and then to the copy shop to have some copies done."

"You aren't going to see Marica, are you?"

This sentence, which I uttered in one breath lest I faltered, marked the point of no return. All the following events were the inevitable consequences of those words of mine.

At that moment the sun was rising. The rays filtered through the window, creating a crown of light around his head. But it wasn't the halo of a saint. Suddenly, the kitchen was filled with light, and all the furniture and objects revived by the colors and shapes that dawn had stolen from them. At that point, I saw it arrive—a punch straight to my nose. Not strong, but well-aimed. I saw the blood gushing copiously all around me; it was on my hands and my night-gown, and all over the floor. Strangely enough, I wasn't feeling any pain.

Because, indeed, nothing had happened.

There had been no punch at all; and no blood. It had just been a hallucination of mine.

"I'll see Marica tonight at the Workshop, with all the other students. And yourself, if you decide to come," he said, flaunting tranquility. But, despite his words, he couldn't hide his irritation.

"The fact is, your mind is haunted by ghosts, Vittoria. I don't even recognize you anymore."

Putting down his cup, he banged it on the table. Then he passed before me, staring me in the eyes, and went to the bathroom to get ready to leave.

TWENTY-THREE

Rome, present day

It's been a week since I met Nadine, and we still have a handful of days together remaining. Try as I might to hide it, she has realized my increasing sorrow at this countdown. She too, although eager to start her doctorate, is equally sad at the thought of leaving. Yesterday afternoon she called the University in Pisa and it seems that they can help her find accommodation. If so, she can remain in Rome until the day before the course begins. Almost another week longer.

"Together till the last minute," she said this morning with a smile, as I was leaving home to head out to work.

We often talk about keeping in touch in the future. But I know how things turn out. Maybe we'll call each other for a while, and we'll meet up somewhere once or twice. Then, the distance will get the better of our friendship, and we'll end up losing sight of each other. But I savor the present moment.

These days, while I'm at work, Nadine walks around the city visiting monuments and museums. Then, around mid-afternoon, she usually leaves the center and goes in search of ethnic food shops, especially in the busy area of Tuscolano. She's got an eclectic taste in ingredients—exotic spices, unfathomable toppings, extravagant veggies. Then, once at home, she combines them all into recipes of her own invention. Calling them *experiments* would be a compliment; the right word is *adventures*. Every night, when I return from work, I find her gastronomic fantasies spread across the table: an array of mini portions in which her French-Italian origins—inflected by her five years in Switzerland—blend with her countless trips across Asia and her obvious innate distaste for conventional flavors.

"Most people don't know that math thrives on creativity; so, when it comes to food, their logical assumption is that I live on bread and water," she told me last night. Whereupon, she served up shrimp pancakes in argan oil, with vanilla ice cream and poppy seeds. My joke at the sight of this culinary extravaganza makes her laugh out loud.

"I think, Nadine, I'd rather eat one of your equations."

We are both so asphyxiated by the ordinary hypocrisy around us, that our bursts of brutal honesty come like a breath of fresh air.

"We'll make up for it tomorrow night," she had replied, without stopping to laugh. "I have a surprise for you that will drive you crazy; I bet you're going to love it!"

Right now, as I leave the Ministry to return home, I imagine Nadine in my kitchen preparing one of her madcap dishes. Rather than her creations, though, I'm looking forward to the fat that we'll chew until late into the night, heedless of the stack of dirty dishes in the sink.

Despite today's double shift, I feel no fatigue. I'm hurrying toward the Colosseum subway station, eager to slip down the subway stairs. In less than forty minutes, we'll be together again, telling each other about our lives, so similar and yet so different: mine—miserable for over forty years—and hers, still budding but already determinedly aiming towards normality, perhaps even serenity. How could this same problem have turned out so differently? The simple answer is that different circumstances lead to different lives. It'd be disingenuous of me, though, to deny that her wit, a cut above mine, trumps all those factors.

Meanwhile, I have made it to the Colosseum station earlier than I expected, and I'm now rushing down the subway stairs. I'm determined to catch the first train, possibly the one that is rattling into the station right now. I swiftly pass through the turnstiles and slip between the doors of the carriage, which close with a sharp bang behind me. As soon as I collapse on the first seat available, I close my eyes, trying to shut out the world from my life. Then, I immediately put on my earphones and start the music on my phone. While the first chords of Borodin's Polovtsian Dances begin to flood my whole being, I think back to my conversation with Nadine, yesterday after dinner.

"Have you ever met anyone like us?" I had asked her, all of a sudden.

As she had lowered her gaze—her smile fading away—I had realized that I had hit the wrong note. However, with a visible effort, she had started to speak. Her first sentence was unsettling enough to make me shiver down my back.

"I can't be sure, Vittoria, but I suspect that my mother was one of us, and the fact that I failed to realize it, overlooking her need for help, is still my greatest regret."

Thus, she told me about her elusive mother, a woman that Nadine had loved immensely despite the wall of mystery that surrounded her at all times.

"You see, my mom was inscrutable to me, just as we are towards each other—an *empty soul*, as you say. Nothing of what she was thinking ever came through to me, nor did I ever sense that a flash was about to arrive from her. And because of this, probably, she was the only person that I always wished to be with. In her presence, I would feel the peacefulness of when I was inside her womb. But it never came to me, until later in time, that it was just this special incommunicability—not unlike ours, Vittoria—that made our bond unique.

"And then there were her weird fights with Dad, which were harsh and frequent. I remember them from childhood due to their strangeness—because they always erupted from a situation of complete quiet. My parents never quarreled over something that the other had said or done. That was the odd thing: I could never understand the reason. Even as I grew old enough to be treated as an adult, both my parents closed themselves off on this matter. Eventually, I convinced myself that there had to be a sort of fundamental incompatibility between them, and I decided not to pry any further.

"One day, on my way back to Arles from Zurich, I found that Mom and Dad were no longer living together. I questioned my mother, trying to fathom the reasons. I insisted like never before, but I failed; she wouldn't tell me anything. Until she got furious and threw me out.

"The next day, I went to see my father, who had moved to a studio flat on the outskirts of the city. When I found him almost in tears, I had the feeling that a flash was about to come. The last thing I would ever want, though, was to enter my father's life. So, I pushed it back down. I raised my mental blackboard against his thoughts. My computations prevailed, but I lost. If I had let the thoughts come, maybe I'd have known more. Maybe I would have understood what had happened between my parents. Instead, as the only memory of that encounter, I'm left with my dad's words: *Your mother lives a difficult life, Nadine. And she deserves all the compassion in the world. But no one can imagine what it means to live with a person who is in your head at all times. Nobody can, because no one else is like her.*

"Two months later, my mother took her own life. A few hours later, my father, upon learning of this, did the same. He could no longer live with her, but he could not imagine a world without her." Finally, I think back to Nadine's closing words.

"Our illness is not contagious. But the ensuing depression can be. For my parents, it was."

Right now, coming out of the subway and heading straight home, I think that tonight I'll give my whole self to distract Nadine from this tragic memory and bring a smile back to her face. I will do my best to redeem myself for my indiscreet curiosity. And, worse, for my blunder of days ago, when I had confessed to her my desire to end it all—to her, whose both parents took their own lives.

As I enter my flat, I find Nadine standing in the hallway. She's smiling, with her raincoat on. I wonder whether she's just got back home or, instead, ready to go out. The other thing I notice is the absence of refined aromas emanating from the kitchen. Lastly, and most strange, Nadine hasn't yet set the table.

"We'll be dining out tonight," she says, with a smile. "We are going to a traditional trattoria: bucatini cacio and pepe and straccetti alla romana as the main course. Or would you rather go for a pajata?"

I remain undecided about how to behave. Shall I pretend to be happy, or shall I disappoint her, confessing my lack of enthusiasm for her plan? Regretfully, realizing that sometimes hypocrisy is necessary, I decide to bear up. After all, she just wants to be kind. So, I mentally prepare myself for hordes of noisy fellow patrons, with enough high-spirited emotion to leave me prostrate, if not unconscious, on the floor.

"It will be just the two of us," Nadine says. "They have a private room, with just one table—ours." So this was the surprise she had planned for me. Without even waiting for my assent, she grabs her phone. "I'm calling a cab," she announces.

Once we get to the trattoria, we order mixed appetizers and straccetti alla romana, as Nadine had suggested. But, rather than the food, it's our feverish talking that keeps our mouths busy. In fact, we give no respite to each other's curiosity, leaving all the dishes virtually untouched.

"Aren't you engaged right now?" I ask her at one point.

"Of course, I am. I'm engaged with disappointments," she replies, with a bitter smile, "I go in no time from the regret of dating one person to the remorse for taking up with someone else, and I consider a moment of joy every pause in between."

"This is what we are both doomed to," I say, thinking back to my few one-night stands from Antonello onwards until I gave up any hope of a relationship.

"And you, Vittoria? Has there been anyone important in your life?" she asks.

I dwell on her question. For a moment, I think I should tell her about Antonello, and everything that followed, but I feel that this is not the right time. And maybe that will never come.

"I had an affair that I thought was important when I was younger than you," I say. "From that moment on, brief relationships only, the last almost thirty years ago. So never, ever ask me any questions about male anatomy because I've no memory of it anymore."

Nadine chuckles.

"Thirty years... without ever wanting to refresh it a bit?" she asks, raising her eyebrows to underline the slyness in her question.

"Thirty years, so far. It's a record that I intend to beat, though." Upon saying that, I'm surprised at myself. My intention was to make Nadine laugh, and I did it. More than that, though, I realize that my words necessarily imply hope for a long life. So, what happened to my stubborn intention to end it all? Where did it go?

When we're back home it's past midnight, and we're hungrier now than when we had stepped into the trattoria. Nadine offers to prepare black Venere rice noodles with ginger oil and soybean sprouts. As I'm far from being sated with our chats, I reply that it's exactly the sort of dish I am craving.

TWENTY-FOUR

March 19, 1978 – Morning

You already know about this early morning. Upon joining Antonello in the kitchen, I had immediately told him that I wasn't well and wanted to visit my mother. That was the truth. It was my actual intention to see my mom as soon as I could. I felt comfort just at the thought of hearing her voice, and I knew that meeting her in person would put my upsets on pause, at least for a few hours. Certainly, I wouldn't tell her about Antonello's affair, nor my suffering; nor, least of all, about that imaginary fist that I had just seen hit my face. Let alone my vision of a wave of blood that, springing from my nose, had flooded all over the floor. Had I told Mom any of that, I would've only increased her disdain for him and alarmed her even more. Instead of finding relief, I would've harvested new and greater pains. Not that leaving all this unspoken would make me completely safe. Like any careful mother, she would've probably sensed something amiss, and I was already prepared for her subtle maneuvers to extract the truth from me. But all these preparations proved to be pointless, because things took an entirely different turn. As you know, my illness was at its earliest stages. Far as I was from grasping its reality, I certainly couldn't use it to my advantage. That morning, therefore, as soon as I heard Antonello close the front door behind him, I went to the bathroom to get ready for a visit to Mom. My image in the mirror, though, made me think again.

Showing up at hers with such a face was out of the question. Only a few minutes earlier, Antonello had said that he no longer recognized me. Now, I could have said the same myself. How could I possibly stand another assessment of this kind? From my mother too? For the third time in the very same morning? I realized that a visit to my mom was a non-starter. With that sick face of mine, aggravated by a night in tears, I would have started such an escalation of mutual anxieties as to depress her and overwhelm me. At that point, I thought that sleep was my only possible refuge and decided to go back to bed.

I woke up at almost 11 a.m. feeling recharged. In front of a cup of coffee, I told myself that if I wanted to climb back to the top, I would have had to drag myself to the source of all my anguish. And that goal—or call it a destination—was within my reach. After all, my anxieties took a concrete form—that of a platinum-blonde and blue-eyed spoiled princess. They also had a name and last name—Marica Beltrami. The only missing clue was her home address. It's true that I myself had registered it when she had enrolled, but that had been almost two months before. While I clearly remembered that she lived in one of Parioli's most luxurious streets, I was uncertain about her house number. For this reason, I came up with the idea of passing by the Workshop; once there, in less than a minute I could check her address. From there, I'd go straight to her house to sort things out. While getting dressed, I tried to work out a plan of dos and don'ts. Especially the don'ts. *Don't make scenes*—I had said to myself—*refrain from insults, hysteria, and self-pity*. To be fair, it was not so much the impropriety of such excesses that restrained me, as their self-defeating nature. Make no mistake—I would have gladly kicked Marica in the shins, calling her names in the street and tearing out her blonde hair by the roots. But all I wanted was to terminate her affair with Antonello, not to offer them the pathetic spectacle of a lunatic—one that would inspire my rival's derision and his ultimate rejection of me. Upon leaving our flat, therefore, I mentally analyzed the risks that my condition implied. On one side there was I, the dogsbody of the school, the cheated-on partner, the ex-belle of the ball; on the other, there was the flowering of a noble scion, with all the allure of a femme fatale: a porcelain-faced doll who would probably receive me in her magnificent living room overlooking Monte Mario—but only after making me wait a good half-hour under the watchful eye of a white-gloved Filipino maid. Enough to make me feel defeated from the outset.

All this notwithstanding, I approached the Workshop in a crescendo of confidence. I thought that I was just making it complicated. As soon as I had found Marica's address, I would walk to her home, and some good ideas would come up along the way. And then, after all, why not simply tell her that I knew about their affair? If I managed to keep my instincts at bay, showing calm and dignity, I would break down her self-confidence. I would undermine the appeal that a young girl might find in an engaged man—that irresistible idea of cuckolding his official partner. But I had plenty of time to refine these details. All I needed right now was Marica Beltrami's home address.

I entered the large room of the Workshop like lightning, aiming straight for my workbench, where the filing cabinet stood.

And there they were. Antonello and Marica.

They were sitting cross-legged on the stage, facing each other. Caught red-handed, they remained still, except slowly turning to me with incredulous looks. During my nightly moments of despair, several times I had imagined catching them *in flagrante*. Not content with that, I had often envisioned them in the most passionate positions of love: the same sexual acts that had been ours, but with Marica's body replacing mine—ardent couplings which, eviscerated of my presence, made my heart bleed. Now, I had caught them in a clandestine encounter—true—but in a state of platonic contemplation. On paper, it should have been less painful. Instead, it was a greater shock. They hadn't met to quickly satiate their baser instincts. No, they were there to be together. They were there because the sex of the nights before had probably satisfied the cravings of their bodies, but not yet those of their hearts. Now, it was no longer human fluids that they wanted to exchange, but feelings, ideas, maybe projects. Perhaps I could have coped with their sexual chemistry, waiting for it to sublimate away. But what could I possibly do against the complicity of two lovers?

As I watched Marica grab her backpack and hurry to the exit, I made a quick inventory of the things that I now had clear in my mind: theirs was not a temporary affair, ours was over, and Antonello would soon punch me in the face. On this last point, I just missed knowing when and where. And, of course, why.

TWENTY-FIVE

Rome, present day

I'm lying down. This is the first and only information that I am sure of as I come to my senses.

My senses. I wonder where they've been all this time. I now feel that they are all regaining their rightful places, one by one, taking the time that they need. Slowly, like an *adagio*, they are retrieving data from my surroundings, to update me on my whereabouts. The first to return is my sense of smell: a pungent and persistent odor of formaldehyde seems to suggest that I'm in hospital. Soon after this, my hearing corroborates and fine-tunes that early assessment: the restless and amplified clamor that I get from around me, combined with feverish footsteps and the acoustic signals of medical equipment, attests that I'm in the corridor of an emergency department. Third comes my sense of touch, which seems to validate all previous suggestions: as I extend my hands in exploration, I find two long metal railings at my sides—the edges of a trolley.

So, there's no doubt: I'm lying on a trolley and I'm in the emergency room of a hospital.

I'm breathing, ergo I'm alive. But at a price. My every breath seems to inhale pain rather than air. Along with my senses, I feel that my memory is also resuming its function, prompted by the question that most presses me—*why am I here?*

A chink opens in my recent memory, retrieving confused shreds of images that chase each other, eager to tell me what happened. Then, slowly becoming clearer and clearer, sharper and sharper, they abandon their evanescent shapes to suddenly acquire the contour of a vivid and brutal reportage.

Metro station, I'm waiting for my train home. It approaches the platform. Why is it so full of people? The turnstiles are just behind me; no chance of escape. The doors of the carriages open with a bang and vomit out its living content. Hordes of people, loud and aggressive, are catapulted out onto the platform. In an instant, I'm surrounded by people. I feel assailed by their urgent needs, fears, phobias, obsessions. A dazzle of colors, a rush of convulsive and overlapping emotions. And then, everything turns black.

Everything turns black. So, here's what happened. I lost consciousness in the subway station. And from there they took me to this emergency room. A place where, with so many people around and all the pain that lingers, I can only feel worse.

This latter thought is sufficient to persuade the one sense that is still missing from the roll-call—my sight—to remain quiet and safe behind my eyelids. I keep my eyes tightly shut. To the point that they start aching. I know that I must keep them as sealed as two gravestones. Each and every image or scene of this place must be kept from my sight. Step back, you place of pain, otherwise I might even die. That's right, I might die. But, after all, isn't that what I've been longing for? Or not? Could I have changed my mind? What kind of event or epiphany could ever make me reconsider that? *Nothing; nothing has that power*, I say to myself. *Who, then? Someone, perhaps?* The faint image of a young woman's sweet visage emerges from my recent memory, pressed by a name that I feel resonating in my mind.

Nadine.

The relief that I feel at recalling her is immediately nullified by the desperation of not having her by my side. Where is Nadine? Will she be at home waiting for me? Does she know that I am here? Meanwhile, I hear the automatic doors of the emergency room suddenly open. Keeping my eyes shut, I hear the wheels of a trolley run fast before me, along with the rapid steps of a large number of people; a man cries out; the soothing words of an old woman are trying to calm him down, while a younger woman is also crying loudly. Something tragic must have happened to these people. I feel for them, indeed I do, but I don't want to live their tragedies. I don't want to. It's unfair for me to enter their pain, and it's not right that it gets into my consciousness. Mutual respect, that's all I ask for.

I think back to Nadine, to her words of a few days ago.

Vittoria, have you ever really fought against your illness?

Fighting my illness? And how, if I don't even know where to start? If I had my music here, at least, I could try. But I don't even have my bag with me.

Wait.

Where is my bag with my phone? Although it has arisen as a concern, I give it credit for distracting me for at least some instants: *what happened to my bag?* The other times I fainted, the ambulance nurses had picked it up and then delivered it to their colleagues at the emergency room. But this time, in that hellish shambles down in the subway, it was probably a thief who took care of it.

Meanwhile, the cries of other patients and the alarmed shouts of the medical staff continuously overlap with each other. The dramas of the former tangle with the urgencies of the latter, and I feel that a wave of pain is about to run over me. *I can't get up. I can't escape. What shall I do?* These are the questions that I ask myself, as I feel my despair mounting.

Under the command of her will, Nadine deploys her army of numbers, equations, impossible calculations. But I—what can I do? What do I know about math?

The automatic doors keep on opening and closing. Doors that let in so much suffering, without letting out a single bit of it. And with this negative balance, I feel that I'm approaching my limit of tolerance. It's a matter of minutes, after which I can only let myself go, yielding to the extreme suffering—the pain of these people around, and everything that can follow.

Wait! Wait! Stop!

A rapid sequence of exhortations reaches my mind, as if another self, inside me, were asking me to resist, to never give up.

I don't know how, nor from where, but an absurd idea is sneaking its way through my thoughts. It's just an idea, and probably it's ridiculous.

But why not give it a try?

If it can't be mathematics.

Could it be poetry?

Poems instead of equations; lines instead of formulas; words instead of numbers. The heart in place of the brain.

'*The Infinite*'. This was the poem that I loved above all others when I was in high school. It was about the universe, and solitude, and despair. But it was about salvation as well, somehow. Reading it always moved me to tears. And as I could never tell those of sorrow from those of joy, I often found myself lost in a three-dimensional maze of emotions—a drawing by Escher but made of thrills, beats, and suggestions.

What if I try to recall the verses of that poem? Is it from here that I can start the passion that Nadine was invoking?

Meanwhile, the automatic doors open once again. I hear the rolling of a trolley being pushed fast, while a nurse is shouting to other colleagues "Quick, quick! To ICU...come on, hurry up, guys... and you move out of the way, you idiot! Faster...faster!"

Always. The first word is *always.*

Here we go...I have it now.

Always dear to me was this lonesome hill

That's how it starts. But then, what follows? Mentally, I repeat the first line once again, and another time, hoping that this will bring me to the second.

Always dear to me was this lonesome hill

But nothing else comes to my mind. I'm here, at a standstill at the first line of a poem; I'm alone on a lonesome hill, beyond which, instead of *The Infinite*, I can find only nothingness.

Meanwhile, the first patient, the one accompanied by the two women, keeps on despairing, inconsolably. His trolley isn't far away from mine—five yards at most—but I feel his sobbing as if it were coming from my own chest. Slowly, his cry of grief starts to shape in my mind—it's the image of a car. It's a white car. I'm at the wheel, and next to me is sitting a child: he's cute and he is smiling at me.

Always dear to me was this lonesome hill

I feel immense love for this child. He's all my life. He's my son, and we're heading to his grandmother's home for lunch.

Always dear to me was this lonesome hill

The car in front of us suddenly brakes. I'm too slow to realize it. An explosion of white hits me in the face: the airbag. In the passenger's seat—blood. Lots of blood.

That's enough, I don't want to see more. It's not from physical pain that this poor man is suffering…I don't want to know more. Mutual respect, that's all I ask for.

… And this hedge, which on so many parts…

The second line. Finally. Here it is.

Always dear to me was this lonesome hill
And this hedge, which on so many parts
Of the distant horizon hides from view.

I wish this were true. I wish that the last horizon were indeed hidden to my gaze. Hidden now, and for my entire life. I wish I could have a secluded hill, all to myself, with a tall, dense hedge. A hedge so intricate and thick as to exclude the entire world from my view. But why am I thinking about this? Why am I not able to stay focused, like Nadine? What are the following verses? What comes next?

I'm now trying to recite *sotto voce* the first stanza. Who knows? Maybe, listening to the lines with my ears, rather than just in my head, can help my memory recall them.

"Always dear to me was this lonesome hill,

And this hedge, which on so many parts

of the distant horizon hides the view…"

Suddenly, I hear the next line come. But from another voice. It's the deep voice of a man that is propelling these words towards my ears. Surely there is a man, right by my side, who is reciting them. Keeping my eyes closed, in silence, I let those loving lines come to my ears.

"… But sitting and admiring endless spaces…"

Who is this man? It's not a familiar voice, yet not entirely new to me. I resist the temptation to open my eyes to discover who he is. I want him to continue, letting my memory recall the missing lines along with him.

"…Beyond that and superhuman / Silence and the deepest stillness…" says the man's voice.

"…and superhuman silence, and the deepest stillness…" I say, just a bit late after him.

"… I conjure into my thought, where / My heart almost scares," we both recite, in the same instant.

My eyes are still closed, about to flood with tears, when I hear the man's voice change tone and turn directly to me.

"It's great to recall 'The Infinite', madam, but…how many more times will I have to take care of your bag?"

I open my eyes. Standing in front of me, in a Red Cross uniform, I see Domenico Morgelli. He has my bag in his hands and a hint of a smile on his face. I can't believe it: the man I had hoped would become my killer turns up, once again, as my savior.

"What time is it?" I ask him on impulse, though conscious of appearing grumpy.

"It's 23.45 right now. It was half-past ten when we came to attend to you in the subway. You were lucky that my ambulance was just outside the station because…"

Morgelli starts reporting details about my incident, but I'm not following him at all. I'm thinking, instead, that my phone in my bag must be gone by now. And, anyway, I don't know Nadine's number by heart.

"Are you still on duty?" I interrupt him, abruptly.

"No, madam, my shift finished after bringing you in."

"Then I have a favor to ask of you. Take a cab to 4 Largo Zuegg, and ring Armieri. Tell the lady who answers the intercom to come here as quickly as she can. Her name is Nadine. The money for the cab is in my purse, inside my bag."

Domenico Morgelli seems puzzled.

"Do you want me to take the money from your bag now?" he asks, uneasily.

"If it suits you, you can wear it as a shoulder bag to the taxi and take the money once you are inside," I reply, dryly.

"May I suggest that I cover the fare; then when you can, you give it back to me."

Upon saying so, he turns around ready to walk away, only to realize that he's still holding my bag. He then comes back and places it by my side, on the trolley.

"Thank you," I say, my tone of voice expressing a kindness that I thought I had lost. Then, I immediately resume, "Forgive my asking, but... we must be the same age, more or less. How is it that you remember 'The Infinite' so well?"

Morgelli spreads his arms, in a gesture of explanation.

"Leopardi was my greatest passion at school, madam..." he says, pausing for a moment.

I keep silent. After all—I think—why should he tell me that he delved into his studies during his twenty-two years in prison?

In the meantime, Morgelli spreads his arms even wider, turning his gesture into an expression of sorrow.

"... and... let's say I had a lot of time to go through it," he concludes. Then, he turns around and walks to the exit.

TWENTY-SIX

March 19, 1978 – Late morning

As soon as Marica grabbed her backpack and left the Workshop, I decided to make myself scarce as well. It took just a second for me to make that decision. But it was long enough to leave upon my memory an everlasting impression—Antonello, with a bewildered look, sitting cross-legged on the floor of the stage. Motionless.

I didn't give him time to react, so I'll never know what was going through his mind. But we can discount the idea of his throwing himself at my feet in apology. Had I stayed, he would have begun instead to enact his usual array of reactions. Passing from gestures of sweet tenderness to indignant silence, he would have inevitably arrived at words and actions of full-blown violence. Until his final victory. He was unsurpassed in this or, perhaps, I excelled in falling for it. Both things, probably. Being the *maestro* that he was, he would have assumed a mask of disdain (*how can you think there's something between me and her?*), then a façade of righteousness, as if it were he who had suffered a wrong (*you lied to me; weren't you supposed to be at your mother's?*). If I had stayed there just one more moment, captured by his gaze, I would never have broken free of it. In the guise of the leading man, he would have used my blind love for him as his stooge. By acting together, shoulder to shoulder, these characters would have turned my tragedy of cheated-on partner into a farce. And any attempt I could make to fight his arguments would have proved counterproductive. Like a consummate actor—the kind of artist who, booed at his performance, finds in the crassness of his audience the confirmation of his genius—he would have called me ungrateful: a thankless young filly, unable to acknowledge his generosity of spirit.

If Antonello didn't start with this pantomime, it was only because I had been faster than him. Lightning quick, I had set off towards the exit, hard on Marica's heels, as if intending to shout abuse at her or pummel her into the sidewalk. But none of that crossed my mind. As I left the building, I burst into tears. I was desperate, but grateful to myself for not collapsing in front of him.

Mechanically, oblivious to the four-mile walk, I headed towards my parents' home. Four miles that I strewed with tears all along the way. Many of the passersby peered at me, some openly, others on the sly, as if to guess the reasons for my despair. Some of them even approached me, perhaps wishing to help me; but the last thing I wanted was the comfort of strangers, especially those motivated by idle curiosity. Walking fast—as fast as I could—was my only chance of escape from those commiserating glances or clumsy attempts to soothe my pain.

When I arrived at my parents' house, they were just about to start lunch. My despondency, already profound, was now burdened by physical exhaustion and lack of breath. When I joined them in the dining room, my state of affliction was such that they refrained from uttering a single word. What could they have said? My tearful eyes, which I hid in my hands, amounted to an admission of guilt and shame. Guilt for shrugging off my parents' misgivings about Antonello and shame for defending him to the extent of fighting with them.

Although my mother knew full well that I would not touch food, she laid a plate for me, attesting her desire to reunite the family. Nor did she expect that I'd confide in them; she just wanted us to be all together and make me feel loved.

Towards the end of their lunch, my father took advantage of the temporary hiatus of tears for a question that I should have seen coming.

"Vicky, has he hit you? Has he?"

With lowered gaze, I shook my head slightly until my shaking became increasingly convulsive and I burst into tears again. Although Antonello's backhanded slap, at the time, had hurt me deeply, the blow of his betrayal pained me more. Somehow my father's straightforward question seemed to merge the two events in my head. I had been hit so hard that my attempt at denial became a tacit admission.

"I don't know what you have in mind," my father said after a few minutes of silence, "but if you think you're going back to pick up your things, well, you won't be going alone."

"Dad, no… I can do that myself," I said, sniffing back my tears, trying to reclaim my status as adult woman.

"Just let me know when you're going, and I'll come along," my father said, resolute.

After my dad went out to work leaving me alone with my mother, I immediately spilled my guts: from the episode of the slap to Antonello's betrayal, I told her everything. Disgracefully, I decided to omit any reference to my perceptions. I thought they were irrelevant to my inner turmoil of the moment. Also, I was afraid they would aggravate my parents' anxiety. My mother listened to me attentively, and at the end of my complaint she asked me abruptly:

"Vicky, do you still love him?"

"I need time, Mom," I replied, after pondering for a few seconds, "but it's not hatred that I feel for him, if that's what you want to know."

"Be honest, with me, Vicky. Are you scared of him?" she asked, looking straight into my eyes. I quickly thought back to my vision of that morning, when in the kitchen of our flat, in a flash of colors, I had grasped Antonello's intention to punch me. For an instant, I saw again before my eyes the blood gushing copiously from my nose and flooding all over the floor.

"No, I'm not scared," I lied, looking away.

That evening, at dinner, I touched food only to move it around my plate, my eyes transfixed on the tablecloth. My parents tried to distract me from my pain by talking of ordinary things. However, it was obvious that my father already knew everything. That became clear at the end of dinner, as we got up to leave the table. My father placed his napkin beside his plate and, turning to me, announced his decision.

"Tomorrow I'm taking the day off. Let me just know what time you want to go."

Then, without leaving me time to argue, away he walked.

TWENTY-SEVEN

Rome, present day

I've been in hospital for four days now, and still no one can tell me when I'll be going home. In these endless hours of confinement to bed, my only moment of solace comes when the orderlies open the doors to visitors, letting them in at last. Just like now.

Mistaken once again for a family member, Nadine greets the nurses in the corridor and enters my room, filling it with her smile. The first thing I notice is that she has removed the scrunchie from her hair. Finally, I can see it falling smoothly over her shoulders, framing her visage with sheen. As she approaches my bed, I feel a pang of joy. Enough to forget, for an instant, that in a matter of days she will be moving to Pisa.

Not even time to greet each other and the head nurse appears at the door beckoning Nadine to follow her along the corridor. While I watch them walk away, my mind goes back to a few days ago, when Nadine had reached me at the emergency room. Morgelli had accompanied her, but I had quickly dismissed him. I wanted to be alone with Nadine and tell her about my experience of just an hour before, when—apparently—I had successfully managed to exclude the pains of others from my consciousness, paying those people the respect they deserved, and gaining in return the peace to which I'm entitled. But, very soon, all my confidence had faded away, and by the time Nadine had approached my trolley, I was more puzzled than ever.

"Is it possible that poetry could have worked for me like math does for you?" I had asked her. "Could it be that the lines of 'The Infinite' are just like parts of a complex equation? Or is it just a coincidence? I've spent my whole life thinking that I have an incurable illness, just waiting for death to end it, and then comes a poem—just a poem—and sets me free? How is that possible? How can I believe such nonsense?" That night, Nadine had listened to my arguments—in which hope mingled with doubt—keeping silent the whole time, as if lost in my words. Then, when I was through, she had smiled soberly. I could read fulfillment on her face, but no joy. I had not found in her gaze the sparkle that I had hoped for: a *eureka* expression as if to mean—*Hey, Vicky, your condition of despair is settled at last.* As soon as she had replied, I understood why.

"You have started resisting, Vittoria. You're mustering up the will to fight. And this is a great step. You have been very good," she had said.

"But then, is it nothing but a step? And what's next?" I had asked her, with a surge of anxiety.

"I don't know, Vittoria. And even if I knew, I'm not sure I should tell you."

I had remained silent, my eyes staring into hers. So, her reluctance to help me was real. That feeling I had had days ago, while she was cutting my hair, was right.

"Why are you dodging my request for advice, Nadine?" I had asked her, trying to avoid sounding petulant.

"Because it's you who must find a way out, Vittoria. If something is going to work, help you get better, it's because you will have found it. And then it's up to you to cultivate it, to make it grow, to turn it into a passion, to make out of it a reason for living, to transform it into something much greater than your illness."

"So, I won't have to repeat 'The Infinite' indefinitely?" I had asked, intending to elicit a smile from her.

"No, Vittoria. I was talking about passions, not obsessions," she had retorted, rebuffing my joke.

In these last days, during her morning visits, I'm taking advantage of the happy opportunity of being alone in my room. Without any qualms, and little by little, I'm revealing to her the saddest and darkest side of my life—my whole story with Antonello. So far, she has abstained from any remark, while her sporadic questions seem to help her put together the various moments of my narration. I appreciate that it's hard for her to find continuity between the naive beauty I had been at the time and today's cynical, ugly old hag; between a girl capable of so much love and an old hermit who harbors bitterness and little else.

Right now, Nadine has come back to my room. She rests her black backpack on a chair and half-sits on my bed.

"Good morning Vittoria. So, a few more days…and then back home, at last!" she utters, taking my hands into hers.

"So, you've talked to the doctors," I say, in an open-ended tone.

"I did. They want to do some more tests, but they plan to send you home as soon as possible: you are fine."

I pull myself up to sit on the bed and silently dwell on her face for a few moments. I'm thinking about how strong our bond has grown in the short space of two weeks. It's not just that I am afforded some respite from my illness when we are together. Nadine is so much more than that. Her words and her gestures flow over my soul like an iron on an old raw dishcloth—smoothing every irregularity, erasing ugly ripples, concealing the frayed fibers, softening the curled hems. To the point that I now start wondering whether this worn-out rag that I am—a rag that I was about to throw into the trash—might have fiber enough to last a little while longer. And perhaps come in handy, if not to me, at least to someone else.

"Look what I brought you," Nadine says, grabbing her backpack and taking out a cosmetics bag. "Today, besides brushing your hair, I'm going to take care of your face. Don't worry—a replenishing treatment with my miracle creams can only do you good; then I'll add a hint—just a tiny hint—of make-up. Are you okay with that?"

While I hear her words without paying them attention, I keep on thinking. There is a question that for some time has been stirring in my mind. *And what if it's her?* What if it's Nadine herself the passion I can nurture to get back to life? For a wreck of a woman like me, with no children or friends, with no relatives or acquaintances, no goals in life except finding a murderer, Nadine *is* indeed life. Isn't she? Instantly, though, another question—a malevolent one—starts pressing me: *why would she ever bond with me?* What do I have to give her? In fact, it's just a handful of days and then she will be gone to Pisa to start her new life. And we'll both disappear back into our separate existences, as it should be.

"Nadine, you're doing a lot for me. But what am I doing for you?" I ask her, taking her aback.

As if I hadn't spoken at all, Nadine opens her make-up bag and twists her body towards me. Then, she strokes my hair with her fingers, as if to contemplate the job she now has to perform.

"Few things are more harmful to the hair than five days in hospital," she says.

She then begins to untangle my hair with small and delicate brush strokes; just as, simultaneously, her gentle words seem to untie the knots of my soul.

"Vittoria, you have no idea of how many things you're doing for me," Nadine says, as she keeps on brushing my hair. "Just think of the story that you are telling me—a story that, I'm well aware, could have been mine too."

"So, do you want me to continue with it? Do you really want to hear what happens next?"

"I can guess your pain in recalling it, Vittoria, and that's why I don't push you to continue. But if revisiting the past doesn't revive your suffering, then—but only then—I'll be content to listen."

At these words, I feel again the intimacy of childhood, alone with my mother. I would sit in front of a mirror as she dressed my hair, standing behind me. As she did so, she would ask me questions, inviting me to open up to her. Thus, she made me feel like a woman. The attention she paid to my words, coupled with her loving brush strokes, made me believe in magic. In those moments, there were just the two of us, the rest of the world locked out.

Just as with Nadine, in this precise instant.

As I feel the bristles of the brush caressing my scalp, I let myself go. It's about time for me to open up to her.

I then abandon myself to both the pleasure of now and the tragedy of my past. Those two moments come together to lead me into a state of mind, hitherto unknown to me, of serene contemplation. While preparing myself to recall an episode of my life that I had kept secret from everybody, I try to gather in my mind the precise sequence of events. Facts that I had buried in my remote memory, convinced that they would never see the light of day. Forever forgotten by me, and never revealed to a living soul.

TWENTY-EIGHT
March 20, 1978 – Morning

My return to the family home—humiliated and heartbroken as I was—had automatically set back by five years my state of independence, at least in my parents' view. Same fate for my autonomy in making decisions. By going back to sleep in the little room that I had occupied from childhood, not only did I implicitly admit all my errors, but I gave my tacit assent to the rules of the house—first and foremost, that of being an obedient child. When my father decided that he would escort me to Antonello's to collect my things, I had no chance to resist; nodding in silence was the only voluntary gesture that I was allowed to make.

The next morning, upon waking, I found that my mind was already at work, occupied with the practicalities of moving back—a good excuse to distract me from last night's nightmares. During my restless sleep I had repeatedly stretched out my arms in search of Antonello, finding instead, as a chasm into reality, the edge of my bed. During breakfast, sitting alone at the table in the kitchen, a breakdown occurred, the first of the morning. I was making an inventory of all the items I had hoarded at the flat during the eight months of our life together, when a fresh batch of tears started rolling down my face. As every object was a fragment of our shattered story, this task proved to be as painful as living again each second that I had spent with Antonello. Counting my clothes, books, records and various other trinkets, it was a lot of stuff and as many tears. I then concluded that three suitcases would be needed: two from my parents' house, plus the one I had left under our bed. With the addition of my backpack, we would have sorted it out in one trip. My world was about to be shattered, but at least with a single blow.

Around nine-thirty in the morning, Dad and I left the house. With my head down, greeted by my mother like a little schoolgirl, I followed my father's footsteps to his car. The two big wheeled Samsonites that we were pulling behind us, empty as they were, produced a gloomy rumbling on the cobblestone, emphasizing the sadness of the moment. If the end of my relationship with Antonello had to be somehow commemorated, our solemn gait, with that deadly drum roll in the background, seemed to represent the perfect funeral.

Twenty minutes later, we parked right in front of the building. While my father was taking the suitcases out of the trunk, I glanced towards the window of our bedroom. In that moment a sudden pain in my solar plexus left me breathless. It's hard to describe the nature of my fear at that moment. It occurred to me that Antonello and Marica could be in the flat, perhaps still in bed. But that would've been just another painful wound in my heart—already so battered to have become numb. What was weighing down on me, instead, was the idea of such a humiliation in front of my father.

When I got to the intercom, I decided to ring the doorbell to warn Antonello that I was going up to get my things. That would have given him enough time to get dressed and Marica a chance to disappear in the case that she were there. I rang four or five times, but no one answered, to my relief. We took the elevator to the seventh floor, where I opened the front door with my keys. The apartment was exactly as I had left it the morning before, except for a couple of details that immediately caught my attention. The aroma of coffee that I perceived upon entering automatically led my gaze towards the coffee pot resting on the stove. I was about to go and touch it to find confirmation that Antonello had left shortly before, but the sight of the unmade bed drove me straight towards the bedroom. It was wrinkled on the right side only—where Antonello used to sleep. So, he had slept alone. This evidence made my heart skip a beat. I won't deny that I had second thoughts at that moment. An attack of delusional reasoning quickly led me to infer that his affair with Marica was over and to conclude that he still loved me. For a moment, indeed, I convinced myself that he had never stopped loving me.

In the meantime, my father was looking around, inspecting for the first time the flat where I had lived with Antonello for eight months. From the entrance, where he was standing, he gazed at the small kitchen and then peeked into the bedroom. It felt as if he was trying to take in, at a glance, all the things we'd shortly have to be packing into the suitcases.

Instinctively, I moved from the bedroom towards the bathroom, where I kept several of my items, including a blue bathrobe—a gift from my mother—and all my beauty products: soaps, shampoos, creams, plus the countless samples and mini samples that I had accumulated over time with my frequent incursions into cosmetics shop. I somehow regarded them as toy soldiers deployed in spirited defense of my fading beauty. As such, I used to keep them perfectly aligned on the main shelf of the bathroom, which ran under the mirror all along the wall. Once inside, I was astonished. No image could have been more telling in reporting the final capitulation of any residual hope: all my products had been badly pushed away against the two corners of the shelf. At its center—like monuments of his regained freedom—were the symbols of Antonello's virility, his razor, shaving cream and after-shave lotion. As for my samples of creams and perfumes—untidily amassed on top of each other, probably knocked down by a brusque gesture—they were the most eloquent emblem of my vilified femininity. It was at that moment that I started packing. I picked up the samples in handfuls, pushing them into my backpack with gestures of resounding rage. Such was my fury, and so loud, that my father—still standing in the kitchen—probably took it as the starting signal of the move. In fact, upon returning to the bedroom, I found that he had already opened both the suitcases and was pulling out the third one from under the bed.

Just at that moment, the front door opened, and Antonello came in. It was the first time that he and my father had met in person, and among the many ways to celebrate their first meeting, this was by far the most inappropriate. Leaning his hand on the edge of the bed, my dad rose from the floor to find Antonello's long legs before his eyes. Then, once he was fully upright, his gaze traveled a good foot upwards until he met his indignant expression. My father greeted him coldly, but politely. I don't think he expected in return a warm sign of friendship, but at least a nod. Knowing Antonello, I wasn't surprised when he ignored him altogether. In fact, he turned directly to me.

"Why didn't you warn me about this?" he said, in a tone halfway between reproach and irritation.

I didn't answer. Although I knew he was right, I didn't want to humiliate myself in front of my father by giving him explanations. So, I went straight towards the wardrobe. Trying to disguise my shaking hands, I began to pull down my clothes from the hangers, angrily, one by one. From this point on, things unfolded in a convulsive manner, in a crescendo of tension and hostility that anyone but me, with all my useless premonitory visions, would have been able to foresee. Antonello pushed aside my father and strode over to me in front of the wardrobe. Once again, he demanded my attention while I kept yanking my clothes from the hangers and throwing them onto the bed.

"Did you hear what I said? You should have warned me before coming!" he insisted, raising his voice.

"Would anything have changed?" I shouted into his face, wagging a hanger under his nose.

I doubt that Antonello's intention was to talk me out of leaving him. On the contrary, I think he was quite happy to have the flat—and especially his bed—back entirely to himself. His only regret being that he was about to miss the factotum of the school. Perhaps because of this sudden realization, he grabbed the hanger that I was taking down and tried to wrench it from my hand. There was a white silk shirt on that hanger—a gift from my mother and father the previous Christmas. While Antonello was pulling the hanger and I was holding my shirt, the delicate material tore from top to bottom. Under different circumstances, the scene would have incited laughter. Nobody laughed, though. We all remained speechless. That torn shirt represented a fatal wound to a family object, and my father immediately took it as an act of violence against me. In two quick steps he squared up to Antonello and jerked the hanger out of his hand.

"Enough is enough!" he shouted, "Get out of here, now!"

I had never heard anyone turn to Antonello in that tone and I began to fear the consequences.

"This is my home." he replied, "Fuck off out of here!" At the same time, stretching out his hand, he pushed my father back a step.

"Congratulations on your bravery! So, you're able to lay hands on men too, huh? You coward!" Dad yelled, almost spitting in his face.

My father's caustic remark said it all. It implied that he knew about Antonello's assault of his own mother and about the slap he had thrown at me. It affirmed, above all, the truth that hurt Antonello the most—that he was a *coward.*

To calm things down, I stepped in between them, but Antonello was already pouncing on my father. The punch he had intended for him hit me right between my upper lip and my nose. Almost instantly, blood started to gush over my chin and my blouse. The blow had not been strong, but precise. The extensive bloodshed seemed to suggest heavy damage. As Antonello stood motionless in front of me, I stooped to grab my ripped shirt and use it to dab the bleeding. I quickly realized that it was nothing serious; some broken capillaries, nothing more than that.

In those moments, emptied of all the shouting and noise, it seemed that the incident was over. But there was something unreal in the silence around us. When I saw the color drain from Antonello's face, it came natural to me to turn around; only then did I realize what was going on behind me: my father was lying on the ground, curled up on himself, with both hands clenched to his chest. His face was tensed, as if his facial nerves had been severed. All the pain he couldn't scream from his throat was etched upon his face.

He died ten hours later, in the hospital, in front of me and my mother, who had been summoned just in time.

The bullet had hit the target.

Of one of his two killers, I lost sight that very day: Antonello disappeared from my life as quickly as he had broken into it. We had no mutual friends, so there was no aftermath, nor did news about him ever reach me. It was not a slow fading, therefore, but a blunt and definitive exit.

The other killer, that woman who responds to the name of Vittoria Armieri, didn't disappear. That one has stayed before my eyes the whole damn time. Always beside me, always inside me, always in front of me: every minute of my life. From waking in the morning to turning in at night, without ever sparing me of her presence. Always ready to pop up turning my dreams into nightmares, or a rare moment of quiet into torment.

Are you now catching on as to why I wish so badly to die? Do you understand that my desire to end it all is nothing but a thirst for justice?

I seek death, because I'm not entitled to forgiveness. I hope it will be painful, like my father's. I hope it will be bloody, because that's how I deserve it. I want it to be at the hands of a murderer, because I am a murderer too. And I have committed that fatal sin twice: as a degenerate daughter and as an inept seer.

Oh, hateful curse of mine, so useless throughout my life, and unable to save my father's life, I beg that you carry out at least one final duty: to find a hand willing to kill me. So, just at the moment of death, I can say that this disgrace I have endured for so long still made sense somehow.

TWENTY-NINE

Rome, present day

I have kept my eyes closed throughout my narrative.

Now, as I slowly raise my eyelids, I feel as if I were returning home from a faraway galaxy. But this is not home. I'm still in hospital; and there she is, right in front of me—Nadine. Half sitting on my bed, her gaze upon my face, she seems to be exploring it in search of something—maybe some residual traces of my remote journey?

She has listened to my story in complete silence. Meanwhile, she has been taking care of me. After thoroughly brushing and combing my hair, she had switched her attention to my visage, devoting her careful touch to my skin. First, she cleansed it with a cotton pad which smelled of essential oils; after this, she applied a scented cream; it was so pungent that it seemed to sting each of my pores with a pin. Finally, she gently massaged my face, starting from my forehead all the way down to my chin. Her fingertips had danced gently between my cheekbones and my cheeks and, especially, around the contours of my mouth. Here, Nadine had twirled her fingers at the rhythm of my words. Midwife of my recondite thoughts, she helped their painful birth, finally giving life to their full disclosure. At one point, towards the end of my narrative, she had asked me an elaborate question, of which I hadn't missed her secondary aim: taking advantage of my momentary silence she had passed a touch of gloss onto my lips.

"Had there been any sign, in the past or even in more recent times, that your father was suffering from health problems—circulatory problems, anything like that? I mean, were there no symptoms at all of heart disease?" she had asked.

So evident had been her intention to come up with an excuse for me—a justification to absolve me of guilt—that I hadn't even answered her, continuing instead with my story.

Now that I'm done talking and she has finished her work, I'm observing her measured gestures. I watch her put her brush and the various creams back into her make-up bag. You'd say that she is completely absorbed in her thoughts, but I've learned to understand this attitude of hers: hiding her disagreement is her way of explicitly manifesting it.

"Were you actually listening to my story?" I ask her, in a slightly offended tone.

"I haven't missed a single word," she replies, darting her gaze over to me. "I'm just ignoring your interpretation of the facts."

We both remain silent for a few seconds. Then Nadine utters these sharp words in her usual tolerant tone.

"Vittoria, you see guilt where there's nothing but fortuity."

Although she knows that my parents and all my dearest friends used to call me *Vicky*, she keeps on referring to me as *Vittoria*. Today, however, after I have revealed to her such personal matters, I begin to feel the weight of that.

"Can't you just call me Vicky?" I ask her.

I realize that the acidity of my tone is entirely unjustified. "I'm sorry, Nadine. In recalling my youth, I've ended up deluding myself that I'm still young. *Vittoria* is perfectly fine."

She's about to reply, but she suddenly turns to the door, because someone is coming in.

"Hello, Domenico," Nadine says, approaching the new visitor with a broad smile. As soon as I see Morgelli enter the room, it occurs to me that on the night of my collapse he had paid for the taxi to pick up Nadine, and I still owe him the money. How inconsiderate of me, I say to myself. Especially towards this man who struggles to make ends meet.

"Sorry, Domenico, for forgetting to reimburse you for the taxi," I say to him, after a quick hello. Then, I immediately turn to Nadine: "Would you please pass my handbag."

"I appreciate that you automatically relate me to your handbag, madam," says Morgelli, giggling with Nadine at his own joke, "but today I'm here for another reason." Upon saying this, he approaches the bed and produces from behind his back a thick and worn-out tome.

"This is all of Leopardi's poems—a textbook from my high-school days," he adds with a melancholic smile. After handing me the volume, he extends his arm to shake hands, and—try as I might to avoid it—I cannot help but think of his crime forty years before.

"This is the third time I must thank you," I tell him, eager to quickly kick out the onslaught of negativity that I feel approaching.

"Nothing to be thankful for. Unless you want to thank me for what I'm about to say: today, madam, you're just as charming as Leopardi's Silvia."

"You mean the young, enchanting Silvia he fell in love with, or the three-hundred-year-old crone she would be if she were still alive?" I retort, taking up Domenico's joke.

We all laugh, and Morgelli, who is in good spirits, doesn't let up.

"Believe me, madam, if I knew that the hospital would do as much for me as it has for you, I would throw myself under the wheels of the nearest ambulance right away," he teases, smiling, first at me, and then turning to Nadine.

An hour later, Morgelli waves us goodbye, and I gaze out of the window; the dying sunset is announcing that it's about time for all visitors to leave. Although I'm exhausted, I feel the urge to go back to Nadine's words: *you see guilt where there's nothing but fortuity.* That's what she had said. Before this, though, I'd like to shed light on a couple of things: was Nadine aware that Morgelli would have come today? And why, upon his leaving, did she ask him to come and pick us up on the day of my discharge? What would be the point of having him here? Can't we just take a taxi to get home? But Nadine doesn't give me time to ask any questions. She returns to half-sit on my bed, this time even closer to me; then, after taking Leopardi's book of poems from my bedside table, she decides how to bring up the subject.

"Domenico is indeed a special person. He has an uncommon sensitivity towards others, and towards you in particular," she says, flipping through the voluminous book.

"How come you have become such intimate friends? You know what this man did, don't you?" I ask her, coldly.

"Of course I know what he did. Once he fought a thief for your handbag; and five days ago, he and his ambulance saved your life."

"That is recent history," I retort. "I'm talking about what he did forty years ago."

Nadine calmly replaces the book on my bedside table. Then she slowly turns to me, staring at me for an instant before replying.

"Okay Vittoria, and so what? Does the fact that he killed two people forty years ago make him a murderer for his whole life? Aren't his twenty-two years in prison enough? And what about his exemplary life ever since?"

"I'm not condemning him again; it just kind of annoys me that you treat him like an old friend of yours."

"Vittoria, let's talk about you, then. You say you're guilty of your father's death, yes? So why should I be friends with you?"

"It's not exactly the same kind of crime, mine and his," I promptly reply, without hiding my vexation for her harsh tone.

"Of course it isn't: Domenico had been betrayed by his fiancée and his best friend, while what were your reasons, exactly, Vittoria?"

Her words are the strongest she has ever spoken to me, and she seems to realize it, because she immediately switches to a softer tone.

"Vittoria, you're right to say that the two cases are different.

They aren't even comparable. But there's something they do have in common: both happened four decades ago. Both of you, albeit in different ways, have atoned for your guilt, or what you consider as such. Don't you think, Vittoria, that it's time to treat him, and yourself too, with a little kindness? Or are you going to blame yourself for your mother's death as well? Do you really think I don't know where you're going with this story?"

"Actually, that's exactly what happened. Who else killed her but me? First, I deprived her of her husband, then of her speech and finally of her own life" I say, interrupting Nadine's complaint.

There are still a few minutes before the nurses come to put out the lights. It will be enough time for me to share with her also this tragic episode of my unfortunate life. Then I doubt she will still speak of *fortuity.*

THIRTY

1978 – March to July

From the moment I came home from the funeral, I suspected that my family's tragedy wouldn't end just with the loss of my dad. My mother's sudden muteness, which began the instant the doctors pronounced my father's death, proved to be much more than a temporary escape from her sorrow.

Upon returning from the funeral service, after crossing the threshold, she hugged me. She held on to me for several minutes, without uttering a word. Then, we went to our respective bedrooms to continue in solitude our ordeal of pain. That same night, at dinner, Mom rejected all my attempts to talk with her. After two days of her obstinate silence, I started to become concerned, but refrained from pressuring her. This somehow implied that I stopped speaking to her. Being just the two of us at home, silence became the rule—and the ruler—of the house. At that time—two weeks after my father's death—I was still confident that once she had overcome her period of deep mourning, she would recover and resume a normal existence. A sad and desperate life, of course, as it can be for a widow who has lost the love of her life, but nevertheless a normal existence.

Exactly a month after the funeral, I woke up thirsty in the middle of the night. As I was heading to the kitchen for a glass of water, I heard a whisper come from my mother's room. I sneaked in and found her knelt by her bed with folded hands. Hearing her murmur *Hail Mary* was a double shock to me; the woman I knew to be an agnostic and who—along with my father, a staunch atheist—had raised me away from churches and bedtime prayers, was now seeking refuge in God. Even more worryingly, I was now certain that her daytime mutism was deliberate. Her choice to remain silent was a voluntary act.

More and more days passed by, and she still hadn't uttered a single word to me.

From the chores to grocery shopping, it was I who looked after the house, and when the phone rang, it was up to me to answer. If someone was looking for her, whether on the phone or at the doorstep, she would always raise her hand before her distressed face, as if to say *'no, not now, not now'*. One evening, while we were sitting down for dinner, I broke the silence to ask her why she was doing that.

"Mom, is it just to me or to the whole world that you don't want to talk anymore? If it's just to me, I can only agree," I said, "but why not go back to a normal life with others, at least?"

On this occasion she didn't even make the gesture of raising her hand; she lowered her gaze to her plate and, taking her spoon, began to sip her tomato soup.

I convinced myself that she had extended her muteness to everybody just from maternal pity. She held me responsible for my father's death—no doubt about it—and for this reason she could no longer speak to me. It's not that she didn't want to: she just couldn't. Like the loving mother that she still was, though, she didn't want to make that obvious to me. Cutting ties with the whole of humankind was therefore her solution.

To add to my anguish, my mother did not fully understand the extent of my guilt. She wasn't aware that I had neglected all my premonitions, dismissing them as senseless hallucinations. The blame she put on me was that of an accident. She regarded me as an involuntary cause of Dad's death. But unlike her—and better than anyone—I knew that I had been more perpetrator than innocent bystander.

One morning, on my way back home after shopping, I saw that our neighbor was leaving our flat to head back to her apartment. I stopped her to ask if she had been visiting my mother and what she thought about her condition. She said that she had failed to get a single word out of her; she had tried in every way to make her speak, but without getting a single monosyllable. Then, before returning home and closing the door, she paused for a moment to look at me.

"Vicky, are you aware that every time you go shopping, just minutes after you've left the flat, your mother starts screaming? I don't even know if I can call them words, it's a kind of gibberish. And she goes on for several minutes. Mind you, I'm not telling you this because it bothers me. I just thought you ought to know."

I had a neurologist come home and visit her. He did the best he could in the face of her total lack of cooperation. Several other specialists came in succession, but no one could get her to say a word. Among them there was also a psychologist recommended by Giuliano, my doctor friend. She came over many times, but with each visit she seemed to lose confidence.

"I really hope I'm wrong," she said one day as I helped her to the front door, "but just as she has stopped talking, she might soon give up eating."

One night, months later, a whisper from Mom's bedroom woke me up. Upon reaching her, I found her knelt once more at the foot of the bed. That night I decided to approach her to talk to her.

"I wish your prayers would be heard, Mom," I said, through tears. "I wish I could do something for you."

That was when she finally spoke—words that I never wanted to hear.

"You pray too, please," she said, "pray that I may die soon."

I stayed by her until I collapsed asleep on the floor. In the early hours of the morning, I awoke and saw her where I had left her, as if she had spent all night praying at the foot of the bed.

A few weeks later, as we were sitting on the couch, her pain materialized in front of me, as if it were oozing from her body.

I saw her lying on her bed, while next to her a young woman handed her a glass with liquid; my mother drank it all and then her head fell backwards, her eyes wide open.

That young woman with the glass was me.

It took another three months of her muteness and of common suffering. Three months of her growing despondency and my struggling despair, but in the end that was exactly what happened. One evening in late July, after several weeks bedridden, refusing water and food, I put an end to her suffering. It was not poison in a glass, but an injection of insulin, compassionately procured by a nurse.

***

"That's all, Nadine.

You know everything, now.

After causing my father's death, I killed my mother too.

Maybe now you can understand why I feel guilt.

Of course, I am guilty.

All right, I'm not going back to that.

Promise.

Let's do as you say.

I'm really very tired now, though.

I'm very sleepy.

Too sleepy to talk.

And it's time for you to go.

Good night, Nadine.

Thank you.

Thank you for listening to me."

FOURTH

Redeeming

THIRTY-ONE

Rome, present day

When I wake up, they're both standing in front of me. Rather than their white coats—actually, blinding—it's their puzzled looks that draw my attention.

They're the two doctors who have visited me every morning from the moment I was taken to this department. The younger one, a handsome guy with a bushy beard and black eyes, has never uttered a single word so far; nor so much as cleared his throat. He must be so freshly graduated that if diplomas had a scent, you would smell it on him—pervasive and persistent like patchouli. The other man, grizzled and bespectacled, exudes instead the seniority required of a doctor who is holding in their hands your test results. While observing this odd pair, I can't help wondering if they are going to be two white doves—messengers of good news—or, instead, two ravens in disguise. Meanwhile, the older doctor raises his gaze from the rustling papers in his hands and exchanges a meaningful look with his colleague. Then, he finally turns to me.

"So, Mrs. Armieri, how are we doing today?"

"I'd say that you're both magnificent…"

Another exchange of glances between the two. Probably they didn't appreciate my witty remark. I wonder how many times they must have heard this same stupid joke by other patients. But if they are fed up with it, why do they keep asking, "How are we doing?" instead of "How are you doing?" Or, perhaps, they didn't like my joke because there's nothing to joke about. Maybe they have some unpleasant news and they're trying to find the most appropriate words. For decades, all my tests have been negative; no wonder something bad has come at last.

Bad? Wait—would it really be that bad?

After all, I'm struggling to find someone to kill me. Isn't an incurable disease nothing but a murderer? My death would be equally painful, as I wish it to be; so, I'd achieve my goal anyway. What difference would it make? My million euros could go to cancer research. Chances are that I would end up no less a philanthropist: go figure.

The older doctor clears his throat. I take his embarrassment as confirmation that bad news is on its way and I prepare for the worst.

"Nothing to worry about, Mrs. Armieri. All your results are normal. By the way, congratulations on that. We rarely come across such flawless test results in patients over sixty."

I keep staring at the doctor without commenting. I'm waiting for his *"But"*—or related expression—that will overturn all that he has just said.

"There's a very slight fracture of the fifth vertebra on your right side, as you already know, but things are progressing well. A few more days of rest at home and, if you don't strain yourself, everything will be fine."

I'm still waiting for his *"But"* to come. It seems I must bear with him a little longer, though.

"Since we've found no pathologies or remarkable abnormalities, it appears that your fainting was just a chance event caused by the circumstances; in short, it might just have been a panic attack."

"... But..." I throw in, urging the doctor to come out with it.

"Yes, you're right: there is a *but*. One of our nurses previously worked in another hospital, and she remembers having already admitted you some time ago, when you had fainted in quite similar circumstances."

"That's possible," I confirm.

"My colleague here…" he continues, "has carried out some research across the various hospitals in Rome, including private clinics…"

He then nudges at the black-bearded doctor, whose voice I will hear at last.

"Mrs. Armieri, our records show that you have been attended or hospitalized for fainting in public places eighteen times in the last three years alone. Is this the case, Mrs. Armieri?"

I notice his tone of voice, relaxed and varied, consistent with a character that I perceive as conciliatory and harmonious. His beard is so thick and dark as to hide his lips almost completely. Too bad—I say to myself—because they must be full and beautifully designed.

"I don't know; I don't keep a precise track," I say, thinking that he must be pretty close to the truth.

The young doctor, meanwhile, resumes talking.

"The fact is, each time you have refused treatment for these episodes. Would you please tell us why?"

"Those drugs make me feel worse," I reply. And I've told him the truth; sedation exacerbates my phenomena both in frequency and intensity. However, I decide to keep this last observation to myself; I have no desire to be moved straight to the psychiatric ward.

"Worse, you say? Worse than dying in a stampede, like five days ago? Do you know that it's only by chance that you're still alive?"

"When can I go back home?" I ask him sharply, deciding to cut to the chase. Nadine is going to stay in Rome for just a few days more, and I can't let them go to waste.

"We're going to discharge you tomorrow, but if you keep refusing treatment, it'll just be goodbye until the next time," he replies.

The authoritative tone of his reprimand, equally gentle and severe, makes me see his callowness in a new light. Then, perhaps feeling he has gone too far, he switches to smooth-talking me.

"You don't want to die, Mrs. Armieri, do you?"

"No, of course I don't," I say, astonished at my own words. Clearly, it would indeed be insane to trumpet my craving for death in front of medical personnel; however, I'm surprised at how convincing I sound.

"Great, then you'll have to stick to an adequate course of treatment. Yesterday, on the phone, I explained the situation to your daughter, and I made her promise that she would persuade you of its importance. That's the best we can do," he says in a definitive tone.

Such is my shock in listening to his words, that I can't find the breath to reply. Not only does he believe that Nadine is my daughter, but he has prevailed upon her to give me drugs.

Just as the two doctors exchange a definitive nod of approval, Nadine appears at the door. They beckon her in and simultaneously move a few steps towards her. As they start small-talking a few yards from me, I wonder how these doctors can possibly mistake me for her mother; what similarities can they find between her young and delicate beauty and my wrinkled, senile features?

As soon as Nadine and I are left alone, I feel I must firmly oppose any medical therapy. But as she's just arrived, I think she first deserves a smile.

"They think you're my daughter," I say, in a complicit tone.

"And let them believe it; at least it's easier for me to have access that way."

"Sure, I just wonder… how can they think such a thing?"

"Well, we're identical, Vittoria. Have you forgotten?"

We chuckle for a moment, then I put on a serious face.

"Nadine, what's this about your promise to the doctors? I mean… that I should start therapy?" I ask her, with no other preamble.

I follow her with my gaze as she turns around my bed and rests her backpack on the chair.

"Vittoria, what the doctors said is true. I mean, I agree with them that you have to start treatment."

I turn to her in disbelief.

"Nadine, do you really want me to start meds? You know how badly they might hurt me, don't you?"

"Who talked about drugs? *They* might have. I certainly didn't."

I'm about to ask her what she means, but she resumes talking.

"Listen to me Vittoria: tomorrow you're going back home, and we still have a whole week together…"

"A whole week, Nadine? Really?" I reply in joyful disbelief.

"Yes, Vittoria, this is the first good news: another student from Zurich has offered me a flat-share, so there's no rush for me to go to Pisa. I can stay here until the doctorate begins. And the other good news is that there is no bad news."

"Well, nothing sounds worse news to me than therapy."

"Vittoria, I promise that before I leave, I will tell you what I mean by *therapy*; but until then, don't ask me more questions. Can I rely on you?"

Instead of replying, I remain silent. I think back to last night, when I told her about my mom: a secret I had never confided to anyone. She had listened quietly the whole time. Half-sitting on my bed, she had never interrupted me. And I was scared of that vacuum of words, so similar to my mother's silence. Was Nadine, deep inside, blaming me? Was she perhaps so disgusted to refrain from commenting? Then, when I was through with my story—and about to faint from exhaustion—I had felt her standing up from my bed. I was sure that she was about to leave because I deserve nothing but contempt. But then, just on the edge of sleep, I felt her fingers on my left cheek. A gesture so remote in my memory that it took me more than a moment to identify it as a caress. How long had it been since I had felt it? So many years, that I had forgotten its wizardry—the superpower hidden in our hands. In my incipient sleep, her delicate touch had turned into words: *Rest now, no more suffering, I love you, I will help you heal.* And then, these words had become images: vast expanses of flowers, clear skies, places of peace, sanctuaries of bliss; places that I perceived with all my senses, as if I were indeed there: walking along those meadows, breathing that purity, feeling the energy of nature, enjoying my freedom.

And now, right now, Nadine is asking me if she can count on me. I'd love to find the most convincing words to express the trust I have in her. And I'm still in search of those words when I hear her speak.

"Anyway, from this moment on, I'll call you *Vicky*," she says, widening her smile.

"That makes me very happy, Nadine. Really."

"Wait, take a look at why." Upon saying this, she opens the side zipper of her backpack and pulls out a small object. It's flat and round, the size of a powder case. I almost immediately recognize it as a purse mirror. As she snaps it open, I instinctively shut my eyes tightly and turn my head to the other side. But I feel Nadine's hand reaching out. She brushes my chin and gently guides my face back towards the mirror.

Then, two things happen simultaneously: I see a reflection that seems to come from my past, and I hear Nadine's playful words.

"You're absolutely right, Vicky: how could they possibly think that such a youthful woman could be my mother?"

THIRTY-TWO

It's five o'clock in the morning, and I'm lying in the semi-darkness of my hospital room. I've been awake for at least an hour, staring wide-eyed at the uncertain shapes in my sparsely furnished environment.

I'm not sure why I woke so early. Is it perhaps because I can't wait to leave this hospital? That's possible, but it might take some five hours before they're ready to discharge me. Or is it because of what I saw in Nadine's mirror yesterday? Then, another question is pressing upon my mind: did that event really happen? Or did I just dream it during the night? Only another mirror can tell me that—the one in the bathroom.

The fact is, I feel caught between a past that I dread and a future which I'm not sure exists, and my thoughts are lurching feverishly from the one to the other—desperately searching for a thread of continuity. Yet, a connection between all the dots exists, and it has a name—Nadine. After all, isn't everything that has happened to me in the recent weeks related to her?

Nadine.

It's not just the doctors: everyone here at the hospital is convinced that she's my daughter. But it's a false assumption. They're misled by the age gap between us and by her constant attentiveness. But they are wrong—twice wrong. Not only am I not her biological mother, which is a given. The opposite is also true: she's like a caring mother to me; and I'm like a child to her. I'm the object of her maternal attentions. A new Vittoria is being born: a woman who is returning to trust people and sometimes even to smile at them. This newborn Vittoria is the fruit of Nadine's womb. Who, but she, is bringing me back to life? Who, if not she, is looking after me with such tenderness? Even when it comes to plans for my future (because it doesn't escape me that she's at that too), she carries them out with the solicitude of a careful mother. Working behind the scenes, she goes straight to her objective—to make me independent, so that I can find my own way in life.

Right now, I feel my body burdened by six nights in hospital, but so eager am I to find certainties, that I gather from my muscles and my will enough energy to get up. To my surprise, my first steps are steady—much steadier and stronger than I could possibly hope.

As I approach the bathroom, I turn on the light and step over the threshold, avoiding to my left the large, square mirror above the sink. I resist the temptation to look straight away at my reflection. Just the thought of it scares me stiff. What if Nadine's mirror lied to me yesterday? What if it deceived me? What if *I* am deluding *myself*?

Carefully, from the corner of my eye, I glance towards the mirror. I'm as much eager to see my face as I'm terrified.

A woman's profile slowly enters my field of vision. She's of a certain age. I can discern her silvery hair, cut short, just above the shoulder. Her forehead is high and rounded. Her nose is sharp. The jawline is soft and feminine. The chin is slightly uplifted. Reassured by these faint clues, I slowly begin to turn to the mirror. Until I come to my eyes. Such a long time has passed since I last looked into them, that their azure comes like a jolt to my faraway memory. *But the hell with the past*—I want to stay in the present. Taking a full view of my face, I notice the remnants of Nadine's artistry—a pale shadow of lipstick remains, while my hair is now disheveled by a night's sleep. Yet, this is the same woman I saw in her mirror yesterday. No doubts. I think back to her words of that moment.

"So, Vicky, do you recognize anyone?" she had asked me, while holding in front of me her purse mirror. Astonished, I had remained silent. I couldn't coordinate a response. Of course, I did recognize someone in that reflected image. Sure, I did. Tucked away among the small wrinkles there was the gaze of my youth. Behind the signs of senility—the natural consequence of the decades that have passed—I had found reflected the allure of my girlhood. Within that little glass—especially—I had found the woman I had been destined to be if my life had not taken its tragic turn. I had seen a face aged by the passing years, but free from all my misfortunes. Not a trace there of my story with Antonello, nor of my fatal passion for him. No mark of the ensuing death of my parents, nor of the pain that followed. No sign of the acrimony that I have accumulated throughout the years. Such had been my astonishment that—with tremulous disbelief—I had managed to whisper just one word.

"Vittoria," I had said, my lips barely moving—hesitant, as if they themselves were surprised at saying my name.

"Vittoria," I'm repeating right now, perhaps even more astonished. Because if the news yesterday's mirror had brought me seemed far-fetched, I have just found its corroboration.

"Vittoria," I say, lost in my reflection.

I'm so hooked on that image of myself that I can't avert my gaze. What I'm experiencing now is quite different from yesterday, though. I'm no more amazed at my regained looks, but at the things I have finally lost. The anger, the rage that I was nursing inside—and that, undaunted, stole insidiously onto my face—has now faded away. I look for it, and I look for it again in my mirrored face. I frown, mimicking its appearance. I curl my lip in disgust, I wrinkle my nose as if smelling something bad, but all I get in return is a good laugh, just as when, as a child, I grimaced at the mirror in jest. And while smiling to myself, I wonder what happened to my impatience, that sense of revulsion towards others that, embodied in a surly countenance, kept everyone at arms' length. It seems to have evaporated. And I don't miss it one bit.

I turn off the light and go back to the room. The first rays of dawn are peeping through the window. Instead of going back to bed, I decide to put on my dressing gown. Then, I take Leopardi's poems—Morgelli's voluminous gift—and walk to the corridor of the department. The nurses will be coming in a few minutes, and after that the doctors will visit me one last time. In just a few steps, I reach the visitors' room, the one halfway between my room and the elevators; a vantage point to keep an eye on the bustle of hospital life. There's someone whom I hope I can meet, this morning. Someone I'd like to talk to. As I reach the visitors' room, I sit on the sofa and open the volume at random, finding the first verses of Leopardi's '*Calm after the storm*', another favorite of mine back in high school.

> *The storm has passed:*
> *I can hear the birds rejoice, and the hen,*
> *Now back to the path,*
> *Chatters and cackles again. Blue turn the skies,*
> *Breaking in from the west, up to the heights;*

With a soft gesture, I close the book and try to recall how the poem continues. The words come to my mind in snatches, the lines, limping uncertain, try to emerge from my memory; several times I must reopen the volume to help me remember. When I get to the end of the poem, at the last line, I feel that the tide of emotions that has welled up in my chest is now ready to spill over as tears.

I'm about to start weeping profusely, but from the back of the large hall I see a white coat approaching—the very person I was waiting for. I watch him coming forward with his brisk and resolute gait, consistent with his slender, athletic build. I quickly wipe my eyes and go to meet him, smiling. Upon recognizing me, he takes his hands from his coat pockets and smiles.

"Good morning, Mrs. Armieri; no better day than the day you return home…"

"You're absolutely right, Dr…"

"Conetrali, Amedeo Conetrali," he replies, rocking on his toes.

"Oh, perfect, Dr. Conetrali... Can I have a minute of your time?"

"Of course, please go ahead."

"To get to the point... I'm not sure if you remember my daughter...?"

"I certainly do," he replies readily. A little too readily, so that I smile inside.

"Well, this morning my daughter is coming to pick me up along with a family friend, and she'd really like to have a chat with you about my therapy before I'm discharged. Would that be possible?"

"I'll be more than happy to do so; I'm going to be in the ward all morning."

"Thank you, Dr. Conetrali; thank you very much."

His black beard ripples on his cheeks to make room for a broad smile, and I take advantage of this hint of approachability to forward my request.

"May I also ask you, if it's not against hospital rules, for your phone number? I promise that I will only use it in an emergency, ... if I were sick or if the meds caused me some issues."

"Absolutely no problem. If you just want to take note..."

"Well... I have nothing on me to write it down. Also, I'd rather you give it directly to my daughter... you know, she's the woman of numbers," I say, cutting off my sentence to pique his curiosity.

"Numbers...in what sense?" he asks, predictably.

"Well, that was just a joke: but it's somewhat true, because Nadine is a mathematician."

"Ah, okay, got it. So, she's a teacher."

"Well, she's actually a researcher. She graduated in Zurich, and next week she's going to start a doctorate in Pisa, at the Normale."

"The Normale!" he utters, in astonishment. "My congratulations, she must be a sort of genius, then."

"You know, Dr Conetrali, more than her talent, it is actually her sensitivity that makes me the proudest. You see, she's the complete opposite of how you might imagine a scientist—cold and unemotional."

"I'm not sure you can take this as a compliment, but from the few words we exchanged, both on the phone and in person, I would never have thought of her as a mathematician. If anything, I'd have said she was an artist."

We laugh together, and since he shows no intention of leaving, I return to the subject.

"As you can imagine, I'm going to miss her a lot."

"I can understand that. From Rome it's a pain of a journey. My aunt and my uncle live in Marina di Pisa, and it takes me at least three hours to go and visit them."

"Ah, so you have relatives in Marina di Pisa…" I say, leaving my sentence suspended in mid-air. My open-ended tone invites him to elaborate and allows me to clarify a bizarre idea that is springing to my mind.

"Yes, that is the seaside of my childhood; and I still go there quite often. Let's say, whenever possible," he replies, playfully assuming a hint of Tuscan inflection.

The seed of my idea, meanwhile, has started to germinate, and although it's still fresh, perhaps premature, I decide that it must see the light of day.

"It's weird that you're talking about Marina di Pisa, because it's there, or thereabouts, that I'm thinking about a second home. A quiet place, close to the sea, where Nadine can go and stay whenever she wants, while I can join her from time to time."

"I can tell your daughter every jot and tittle about Marina di Pisa. All the information she needs."

"I'd be infinitely grateful, Dr. Conetrali."

"Nothing I'd like more! When I talk about those places, I feel like I'm there; so, I do that as often as I can."

As he walks away, turning back for a final nod, I find myself thinking of my life. What would have it been like, if I had fallen in love with a man like that when I was still young? As young as Nadine is now, let's say.

THIRTY-THREE

Ready to leave the hospital, I'm standing at the window of my room. In front of me, a charming November morning is extending its golden reflections over the red roofs of Rome. While I observe the sun's rays toying with the bells of the tall belfry opposite me, I have a distinct feeling that Domenico Morgelli is about to arrive. This time, though, the information doesn't reach me through unwelcome explosions of colors; I've simply combined the time on the belfry clock with Nadine's words yesterday.

"Domenico will come tomorrow morning at nine-twenty-five sharp."

In fact, as I turn to the door, I catch the precise moment of his arrival. Clearing his throat, he shily waves in my direction. I look at his slightly stooped figure: he seems anxious to downsize his body mass, to diminish the bother he thinks he's causing me. What strikes me, though, is his attire: a dark-blue suit and a regimental tie on his light-blue shirt. I can't help wondering whether he's decided to dress up like a limousine chauffeur as he's going to drive me home, or whether he sees my discharge as an event worthy of celebration.

"Good morning, Domenico; thank you for coming," I greet him. It's the first time that I refer to him by name, but, given that Nadine always talks to him like an old friend, I find it appropriate.

"Good morning, madam Vittoria; I'm glad to see you eager to go home," he says, indicating my two bags leaning against the wall. It doesn't escape me that he has reciprocated my "*Domenico*" with "*madam Vittoria*": as familiar as it is respectful. Also, he seems surprised at my being ready to leave. It may be that he had prepared one of his quips about ladies always being late, and now he has got to come up with something different.

"Yes, I just can't wait to get home, Domenico. You're absolutely right."

He continues standing by the door, as if a "*Do Not Disturb*" sign at the handle prevented him from stepping in.

"Nadine said that she would be here by nine o'clock." Upon saying this, he quickly starts looking around, as if his act of searching for Nadine could make her magically appear in the room. Through this gesture of his, indicative of his awkwardness at being alone with me, I get all the genuine simplicity of this man.

I beckon him to come in and offer him a chair, while I go to perch on the edge of my bed, with my gaze in his direction.

"Actually, Nadine did arrive on the dot of nine. She's now at Dr. Conetrali's office sorting out my discharge; she may take a little longer than expected," I say, expressing both a possibility and, deep inside, my real hope. "But you're not in a hurry, are you?" I ask.

"No, not at all, I took the whole day off."

"As a volunteer as well?"

"Oh no," he replies, promptly. "As far as my shift goes, I start tonight at six-thirty. I can skip a day's work, but I'd never miss a single day with my ambulance," he says, raising his eyebrow to emphasize his last sentence.

I realize that in our previous encounters he was always bundled up in his coat or in his volunteer uniform. But today's suit reveals a slender and still agile build, and this explains how he managed to tackle that thief, last month at the park.

In the meantime, Morgelli shifts his gaze to a corner of the ceiling, desperately looking for a new topic to throw into the conversation. I decide to help him out, probably making things worse.

"You're looking dapper, today."

"Thank you, madam Vittoria," he replies, taking my remark as a compliment. "Every now and then I like to dress up a bit, and today… well, I just fancied it." He completes his sentence by twirling his hand a couple of times, to underline the mere randomness of his decision.

"May I ask you what you do for a living?" I inquire, even though I already know it. It's not that I want to put him to the test; I just think it'd be strange not to ask about him. His ready reply proves that he was just hoping for such a simple and straightforward question—something on which he can dwell for a while, easily filling the time until Nadine arrives.

"I work at my cousin's cleaning company; we look after several offices in the EUR area. Let's say I've become kind of his deputy: I coordinate people's shifts…I deal with payrolls, take care of the purchase of the cleaning products…" He leaves the sentence pending and lowers his gaze. His attempt to make a good impression on me is so transparent as to move me. Perhaps he himself realizes that he has given himself too much importance in describing his duties. So much so, that after a moment he resumes talking.

"Mind you, I muck in with the cleaning the same as all the others, though. I never shy from hard work," he concludes, with an outburst of sincerity.

I suddenly feel the urge to be as frank with him as he has been with me.

"I've been cleaning toilets for almost forty years, and I'm quite good at it," I say, in a conclusive tone, to give time for his reaction. As I expected, Morgelli remains speechless. When he resumes, after swallowing the news, his look betrays his embarrassment. Then he gradually starts to unfold his thoughts, until he tries out a smile of relief, as if his effort to put together a good reply is finally rewarded by the words he has found.

"I find it admirable that a woman of your social background has the humility for doing what you do. My congratulations on that, madam Vittoria."

"*My background,* you said? Look, Domenico, I only have a diploma, I haven't even finished my studies. Perhaps it's you who could aspire to something more with your degree. Am I right?"

"How do you know I took a degree?" asks Morgelli, frowning.

"Apologies… it's your knowledge of Leopardi's poetry that led me to think that: a wrong assumption, I guess," is the answer I manage to cobble together.

"The fact is, you're right—I graduated in contemporary literature."

His answer, for reasons that I know full well, is marked by a touch of melancholy. Instead of vibrating with pride, it tolls like a sorrowful admission.

"It seems that you regret it," I say, to encourage him to continue, "yet such a demanding degree should gratify you."

Morgelli closes his eyes and pauses, as if to put together his thoughts. In this brief pause, I'm reminded of Nadine: she's been talking to Dr. Conetrali for forty minutes now, and I'm in no rush to see her come back. Much less at this moment, as Domenico begins again.

"I took my degree while in prison. I've had twenty-two comfortable years at my disposal to complete my studies. It wasn't that hard, in the end; well, I mean, taking my degree."

His candor leaves me stunned. I didn't expect this revelation; not at this juncture, at least. Should Nadine enter the room now, Domenico would be compelled to leave me with nothing but this shameful image of a former convict. I instinctively go to his aid.

"Domenico, there's nothing that I need to know about you, except what might help you feel better."

Upon uttering these words, I realize how both true and false they are: there's indeed nothing I need to know about others; it's false that I have ever tried to make someone feel better.

Morgelli crosses his legs and simultaneously folds his arms in front of him, his biceps swelling in the tight sleeves of his jacket. He's pressing his forearms so hard against his chest that he seems to want to squeeze it, to compress all the weight that it keeps enclosed. With various hesitations, interspersed with gloomy silences, he tells me everything. His voice cracks when he names the two kids he killed forty years ago; he turns his head away as he recalls the triggering moment of his madness, when he surprised Mirella, his girlfriend from childhood, the only woman in his life, in another man's arms on a bench in the city park. He doesn't mention that this young man, Valerio, was one of his best friends. I suspect that this omission is deliberate—in order to reject any extenuating circumstances for himself. The progress of his narration seems to confirm my idea: he admits, in fact, that he hadn't acted just on impulse. He killed them only the following day, after finding them again in that same place. As a consequence, he was convicted of premeditated murder, with a longer sentence in jail, and even greater guilt to carry. "Such immense guilt," he says, "that no period of time will be long enough to erase."

In the seconds of silence that follow, I'm reminded of Nadine's caress two nights ago. Thinking back to the magic of that contact, I now wonder whether a caress can be the carrier of a healthy contagion—as soon as it reaches you, you would like to pass it on to others. Who knows, maybe I would even have reached out for his hand at that moment, and so continued the positive momentum that Nadine had set in motion the other night. But it's she, Nadine, who unintentionally thwarts my aim. At this very moment, in fact, she appears at the door.

Standing on the threshold, she immediately darts a look of reproach straight into my eyes. Well hidden behind her restrained anger, I find the information that I care about the most: the conversation with Amedeo Conetrali went exactly as I had hoped. Reciprocating her gaze, I display an innocent smile—a smirk of complacent contentment. Nadine then turns to Morgelli, shifting from her annoyed look to a sigh of patience.

"Hi Domenico, sorry for being late... not my fault," she says, giving me the evil eye.

"Don't worry, Nadine, we've been keeping each other entertained with a number of topics," I say, hinting at Domenico, "and we could've kept going for hours, couldn't we?" I conclude, trying to play down the situation.

Morgelli, who had already stood up to grab my bags, interrupts his action. Then, turning towards Nadine his impish grin, he flings out his arms in a dramatic gesture.

"Come on, Nadine: you didn't even give us time to go through all of Leopardi's poems."

Bravo, Domenico, I think to myself, noticing that, at least, Nadine has cracked a smile.

THIRTY-FOUR

It's almost eleven o'clock when we step out of the hospital's main door. The late autumn sun seems to be poised there, high in the blue sky, with the very purpose of warmly welcoming my newfound desire to live.

I know my illness is still here, and thriving, inside me. I have no delusions that it will disappear forever. Yet, I feel that it suffers now, at least. It does not succumb, but it falters; it's enduring the defensive blows of this new woman that is me: no longer a passive old lady, but a fierce warrior, armed to the teeth to maim and incapacitate. Perhaps even now it's trying to get the measure of this new version of me; and there's little doubt it will soon return, redoubling its efforts—just to find me even more combative.

Preceding Nadine and Domenico, I go down the steps leading to the large gate, to leave this hospital behind me once and for all. Meanwhile, I gaze again at the clear sky. It's one of those mornings that break free from the season's dictates to do it their own way. If you ignore the autumnal clues—the withered branches on the trees and the yellowed leaves that roll in the breeze—you'd say it's the perfect day to slip into your swimsuit and run straight to the beach, in time for a dip before lunch.

I close my eyes for an instant and breathe deeply. I feel my diaphragm draw the air into my lungs filling them to my nostrils: an involuntary contraction that seems to start from the depths of my body, to capture all the air of which I've been deprived—not so much during five days of hospitalization, but in my whole desperate, cloistered life.

Domenico's amiable tone brings me back to reality.

"You ladies can just wait here for me: I'll just get the car and I'll be back," he says, resting my two bags on the sidewalk.

Nadine watches him walk away. I know that in a moment she will rant at me, calling me a meddling matchmaker. So, I decide to cut to the chase.

"Did he give you his phone number?" I ask her, feigning naivete. In return, I get her narrowed gaze, while a flush blazes upon her cheeks.

"Vittoria, what are you playing at?" she asks, her irritation blatant.

"What's weird about wanting a decent son-in-law?"

"Yeah, right! On top of everything else, you've also told him that you're my mother. It's a lie; don't you realize what a lie that is?"

"Well, I just corroborated an assumption he had already made," I say, with candor. "And by the way, I intend to adopt you, so it's more of a half-lie, so to speak."

"What?!" she exclaims. She actually screams it, drawing the attention of some passersby.

"I want to adopt you. Yes, you got it right."

"But who told you I want to be adopted? Do you think you can do that without my permission? Do you, Vittoria?"

"Vicky. You said you would call me Vicky."

She turns away from me, an evident sign that she's going to get mad, and I can't let that happen. When Morgelli comes back, in a matter of minutes, I want things between us to be straight again.

"If you don't want to, I won't insist upon it. Don't get angry, Nadine," I say, with a hint of dishonesty. I know that I will come back to this point at the right time, one day.

"Do you realize what you have done? Do you understand how you've embarrassed me with that doctor?"

"His name is Amedeo, Amedeo Conetrali," I specify.

"Whatever. Do you understand my embarrassment? Do you?" Nadine insists, harshly.

"What do you mean 'embarrassment'? When you were talking to him the other day, and the day before that, you looked perfectly comfortable. Entirely at ease," I retort, ready to fight back.

"What does that have to do with it? Do you think I can't find a boyfriend on my own, assuming that I ever want one?"

"All right, stop. Forget about it; my apologies," I say, displaying contrition. Then I immediately add: "Cut him loose, end of the matter," I decide to bluff.

"Right, and how am I supposed to end the matter, now that he's got my phone number?"

"Well, you didn't have to give it to him," I reply, coldly.

"Yes, I had to. And the reason is another nonsense of yours. He wants me to get in touch with his aunt, in Marina di Pisa, about the property you want to buy. What is all this about?"

"And you call that 'nonsense'? It's a great idea: a house by the sea, near Pisa, where you can go any time you like. And if you want to put me up, once in a while, we can meet there."

"Yeah, so I should put you up... at your own house?" she blurts out, smirking with sarcasm.

"No, *your* home, because it will belong to you."

"Vittoria, you must have gone crazy, I want nothing from you," she says, casting me a withering look. Then, she suddenly averts her gaze from me, as if she's ready to cut the conversation dead, and perhaps to leave. I have a minute or so to get things right. One minute and just one card left to play.

"Nadine, you asked me what I'm playing at, right? And you, what kind of trick are playing on me? On me and Domenico? Just because I didn't study math, do you think I'm stupid?"

Nadine lowers her gaze, taking the blow. A pause, hers, that allows me to insist.

"When you put make-up on me, the other day, you knew that he was about to come and visit me. Didn't you?"

"What's wrong in looking nice when someone pays you a visit?" she says in a subdued tone, trying to pass it off as an ordinary act of kindness.

"*Looking nice*, you say? By putting lipstick on me? Something I haven't done for more than thirty years?"

Nadine's silence is the sign that I have been able to turn the tables.

"What day is it today? Is it Thursday?" I ask, calmly, feeling that I have taken matters into my own hands.

"Yes, it's Thursday," Nadine nods.

"Well, today is my first day of recovery, then I'll have another day of rest before the weekend."

"I don't get what that has to do with it," says Nadine, bewildered.

"It has everything to do with it because I'll start resting from tomorrow. Right now, instead of heading home, we're all going to the seaside: you, Domenico and me. Fried fish, my treat."

Nadine scrutinizes me, and I sense behind her gaze she's making a calculation. She's analyzing the equation I've proposed to her—a mathematical operation of elementary simplicity. It states that if she wants me to stick to her plans— including the conjectures she's making about me and Domenico—then she has to accept my projects for her future in return: a house in Marina di Pisa and, perhaps, a fiancé here in Rome: a route to happiness, but also for cementing our friendship. I know our rapport has become vital for both of us, and there is no reason in the world that it has to end here. It's a simple calculation to make; for a mastermind like Nadine, it's a no-brainer. However, she takes a few seconds before answering.

"I get it," she nods.

"Great," I say, "Then, do you agree that we all have lunch together by the sea?"

"Yes, I do agree. I got it," she repeats, meekly.

My contentment lies not so much in having her where I want her, but in my belief that she will soon be happier than she can imagine right now.

Domenico's little blue car stops right in front of us: we see him get out and run to open the boot. As he's loading the bags, we get into the car, finding the last opportunity to end our conversation.

"Anyway, you are right," I say, "Domenico is indeed a special person."

From the passenger seat, Nadine turns to me and nods. Then, a moment before Domenico gets inside, she whispers the words that make me beam with joy.

"Vicky, there's something you must tell me, though. How did you know that I like him? Amedeo, I mean."

"Just intuition, Nadine. Nothing but intuition," I answer, keeping a poker face.

Nadine looks at me frowning; my reassurance doesn't seem enough. I raise my hand in front of me and, with a solemn expression, add: "I swear it."

Domenico enters the car and fastens his seat belt. Then, sensing something unusual in our silence, he pauses before turning on the engine.

"Is everything all right?" he asks, shifting his gaze from me to Nadine.

"Well, Domenico…" she jumps in, quickly "… there's a change of plan—if that's okay with you, of course. How about heading to the coast?"

"Come on, Domenico," I tease him, "don't try and tell us that you don't like fish."

He smirks in the rearview mirror and starts the car.

"Between me and fish is mutual love, madam Vittoria. If fish could choose, it would want to be eaten by no other than me."

THIRTY-FIVE

We have persuaded the restaurant's manager to set up a table outside for us. A fitful breeze from the land sometimes overshadows this generous November sun, but we have all agreed that a seafront lunch is worth the trouble. Moreover—being the only customers to brave the weather—we are going to have the whole terrace to ourselves.

We have just placed our orders (mixed fried fish and a bottle of Greco di Tufo) when Nadine's phone rings. I follow her with my gaze as she gets up from the table. I notice that upon answering the call, she heads towards the farthest side of the terrace, which is mostly in shadow. Meanwhile, I already feel Domenico's discomfort at being left alone with me.

"Good that someone has called Nadine," I decide to tease him, "so we can entertain each other with a few lines of 'Le Ricordanze'."

Domenico smiles at my joke, moving his gaze towards the horizon for an instant.

Then, looking back at me, he becomes thoughtful, except for a hint of a smile to the waiter, who has come to let him taste the wine. After a nod of approval, Domenico waits for the man to fill the glasses and, as he walks away, begins to talk.

"I just didn't expect your invitation, madam Vittoria. Usually when people come to know about my past, they duck out as soon as they can, disappearing forever. For this reason, I prefer to let them know from the off. I want them to have the opportunity to make a choice: they can either keep me as a friend, aware of who I am, or discard me forever, for who I once was."

I'm so much struck by his sentence that I find myself repeating it mentally, so as to seal it in my memory: *they can keep me as a friend, aware of who I am, or discard me forever, for who I once was.*

This is an opportunity that I have never given to anyone.

Domenico's sincerity leaves me astonished. It leads me to close in on myself for a moment. Perhaps too long a moment. It's hazardous—my silence—because he could easily misunderstand it. However, I cannot immediately reply to his words. I must first process a whole series of thoughts that overlap with each other in my mind. I'm thinking that I ought to be equally honest with him and tell him everything about me. I should reveal to him, now, right now, that I'm doomed to stick my nose into the lives of others, including his. I should admit that I became aware of his crime the moment I saw him at the park, some two months ago. And that I know more details about it than he can possibly imagine, perhaps more than he knows himself. I should confess to him that I'd weighed him up as a dormant killer to end my life. I ought to tell him that now, thanks to Nadine, I'm fighting with all my might against my illness, and that a few seconds ago, while he was tasting the wine, I have chased away, by an effort of sheer will, all the pernicious feelings that were trying to sneak into my consciousness. I should explain to him that my life is as bad as his, if not worse. Yet, I can't mention any of this to him. I can't tell him—just like I've never been able to tell anyone else. When Domenico confesses to his crime to new acquaintances, he gives them a choice: keep him as a friend or discard him forever. If I were to talk about myself, what choice would I give people? None. I would be just a crazy psychic, a certifiable elder. And no one chooses to be friends with an old madwoman.

Meanwhile, in the background—behind Domenico—I glance at Nadine, with her ear still glued to the phone. She leans her hip against the railing of the terrace and at the same time tries to keep her hair in place, resisting the caress of the breeze. Her body, perhaps due to the chill, shakes briefly. Soon afterward, she laughs a laugh that seems to come from her heart.

I look back to Domenico, focusing my gaze on his broad and honest face, where the signs of melancholy overlie, wrinkle on wrinkle, with those of his age. Yet his countenance, although reflecting the scars of his soul, is always on the hunt for reasons to smile. In Domenico, I see a man who appeals to his every inner resource to bring to the surface the sweet and smooth disposition that he cradles within himself.

"I was thinking of you, Domenico, and of Nadine; I find it curious that I came across you both so close in time. Because the two of you are perhaps the most beautiful things in my adult life," I tell him, all in one breath.

As I finish my sentence, I wonder with a surge of anxiety whether my statement is utterly untimely. Domenico, after all, thinks that I know almost nothing about him: just the few things he has told me. He is ignorant of exactly what and how many aspects of his life I'm actually aware of: his state of deep affliction in the aftermath of his crime, his repentance, his devotion to the cause of the sufferer, his urgency to transmit love and do good to others, and finally the real sense of his passion for poetry, which he has turned into an instrument of redemption. I shudder at the idea that he may consider my remark premature and superficial. Unexpectedly, however, I find relief in his reply.

"This is the first time I have felt understood by someone who barely knows me. And the reason for this can only lie in your extraordinary sensitivity, madam Vittoria."

My curse. Never before had someone called it *sensitivity*.

Domenico lifts his glass, inviting me to do the same.

"On top of that, your putting me beside Nadine is the best compliment I have ever received," he adds.

I decide to take advantage of this remark to switch to a new subject.

"Whom do you think she's talking to?" I ask, with a nod over his shoulder.

Domenico half-turns to observe Nadine behind him. Still on the phone, she's walking parallel to the railing and looking down at her feet, as if she were counting her steps. After studying her for a few seconds, Domenico looks back to me.

"Fifteen minutes standing in the shadows in this wind? Can't say whom she's talking to," he states, "but I'd say Cupid is at work; very little doubt about that."

"Spot on. The winged child seems to be firing arrows like crazy," I confirm.

The arrival of our orders on the table, some minutes later, finally induces Nadine to end her conversation and join us once again.

While she takes from the serving dish a measured portion of mixed fried fish, I search her gaze, finding it as bright as it is absent, as if she were still lost in her last words on the phone. A knowing look that I exchange with Domenico suggests that he has the same feeling.

For a few minutes, we eat in silence. Hunger seems to have joined us at the table as the main guest, preventing us, with its insistent presence, from uttering a single word. Until a second sip of Greco loosens Nadine's tongue.

"It was Amedeo, on the phone," she tosses out, trying to sound natural.

"Amedeo is the doctor at the hospital, Dr. Amedeo Conetrali," I clarify, turning to Domenico.

"Who? That handsome young doctor with the hipster beard?"

"What's a hipster?" I ask, looking from one to the other.

For a moment no one answers, then Nadine turns to Domenico a broad smile, surrounded by a sudden blush.

"Yes, that's him, anyway," she admits. Then, referring to me, she adds: "He said that he has already talked to his aunt in Marina di Pisa. Apparently, she knows of some affordable properties just by the sea."

"Fantastic, this is great news," I exclaim with enthusiasm.

"Amedeo suggests that we go and visit her next weekend, when he will be there too."

"Sounds brilliant. So, you're going to meet him next weekend!" I say, keeping it halfway between a question and a statement.

"We're all going to meet him," Nadine corrects me, laying down her fork. "You and Domenico will be coming too, won't you?"

Nadine's remark does not surprise me in the least: she's reminding me of the clauses of the verbal contract we have signed this morning. Meanwhile, my gaze meets that of Morgelli. I read in his eyes the desperate need for help to understand what's going on.

"Domenico, don't worry, I'll tell you everything later—if you'd like to know, that is. For now, though, let's enjoy our lunch."

But Nadine immediately comes back to me. She speaks very fast, as if, instead of a sentence, she were uttering a single long word.

"I'm probably going to meet Amedeo tomorrow night; you don't mind if I dine with him, do you, Vicky?"

Unlike her, I decide to punctuate my reply word by word.

"On the contrary—I'm overjoyed to hear that. I bet, though, you don't want me and Domenico around this time. Correct, Nadine?"

THIRTY-SIX

This morning, at the end of my convalescence, I have headed straight to my workplace—at the Ministry of Cultural Heritage. At eight-thirty, punctual as ever, I've inserted my badge to pass through the turnstiles reserved for the personnel. Simultaneously, a name has flashed on the digital display: Vittoria Armieri.

Vittoria Armieri?

No, not at all. You must be mistaken, my dear electronic device, I've said to myself upon taking back my badge, *This is Vicky Armieri.*

It took me more than forty years, but I have now returned to being the woman I once was. Although wrapped in today's senility, I have retrieved the sweetness of mind that I once possessed and never wanted to lose. My desire to love and be loved, once so closely bound up with my character, has found its way through the wrinkles of my face. And now it shines through as an aged youth or, if you prefer, as a revived senescence.

Ever since that night at the emergency room, I have managed to resist the attacks of my illness. When I feel its outbursts approaching, I start gathering the strength to fight them. Just as an exorcist wields the crucifix in a mix of fear and courage, I pull out my poor arsenal. It's just makeshift weapons, badly sharpened, and I'm a novice. Yet, I have begun to use them. I now leverage my will—which *wins over everything*, as Nadine says. I now unsheathe all my love for her as an instrument to save us both. I can't allow the goals I have achieved with her to go to

211

waste. I won't any longer admit to my presence that obnoxious old woman that I once was. I'm not letting that crotchety old broad resurrect her old desire for death. To prevent all of this from happening, fighting hard might not suffice. That's why I've decided that I'm going to devote myself to this purpose.

This morning, like every working day for thirty-seven years, I have taken the lift here at the Ministry. But today, instead of heading to the locker room, I'm going straight to the third floor. Walking along a never-ending corridor, among majestic Renaissance paintings, I'm now reaching the HR department. It's my intention to talk to the assistant to Emiliano Reggi, one of the bosses. But there's a better opportunity. I come across Emiliano Reggi himself right now, just as he is coming out of his office, holding some papers.

"Good morning Mr. Reggi, how are you?" I greet him courteously.

He's a meek man, an unusual quality for someone with such a role in a public office. In fact, he reached this position due to quite different reasons, but I do not intend to talk about them. I don't even want to be reminded of those reasons. It's his business. Not yours and especially not mine.

"Good morning madam, how can I help you?" he asks, addressing me as a stranger. And yet, thirty-seven years ago, when I first grabbed broom and bucket, he was already a supervisor here at the Ministry. For a time, before he moved up the ladder, he even used to greet me. I well remember his mischievous glances at my legs when he walked into a toilet and found me there, bent down to clean the floor.

"Well, I'm here to resign," I say, in a friendly but decided tone. As I see him hesitate, I'm tempted to help him out, but the singularity of the scene holds me back. What's the harm, after all, in enjoying a moment like this?

"You… do you work here?" he finally stutters.

"For almost forty years. I am Vittoria Armieri, of the toilet service," I reply, waving my forefinger up and down to indicate the floors.

I'm hardly surprised by his reaction—a look of bewilderment steals across his face. It's somewhat reminiscent of my next-door neighbor's incredulous gaze last Thursday. It happened in the lobby of my building: Nadine, Domenico, and I had just returned from our lunch at the seaside and were waiting for the lift; when it arrived, my neighbor came out of it, and she was petrified. I might as well have been the Medusa. Judging from her face, since she knew I had been hospitalized, she must have thought I had gone there for plastic surgery.

Even Emiliano Reggi, at this moment, seems to have lost command of his facial muscles. In his defense, I must admit that my Saturday shopping spree among the fashion boutiques of Via Condotti has yielded an unusual outfit for a cleaning lady, to say the least. That afternoon, Nadine and I had left home in search of a little boost to my wardrobe. When we came back, late at night, the taxi driver couldn't stop pulling boutique bags out of the trunk. The fact is, I'm now wearing a black boiled-wool coat over an anthracite silk outfit: a black-on-dark juxtaposition strictly imposed by Nadine *for safety purposes*. In any case, there's no better day to show up at work smartly dressed. I believe that the first resignation of my life, after thirty-seven years of service, deserves special treatment.

"Mrs. Armieri, apologies for not, well, recognizing you… but… what's going on?" Reggi stammers, his eyes darting up and down my body.

I choose to misunderstand, voluntarily, the sense of his question.

"I think I've worked long enough; it's time for me to retire. This is my resignation," I say, handing him a letter.

I watch him put on his glasses and quickly review the three lines I've written by hand.

"Well… congratulations indeed, Mrs. Armieri," he mutters, bringing his eyes back to my person.

"It's just a letter of resignation," I say, raising my eyebrows, although it's quite clear that the compliments were not directed at my calligraphy.

"Great… the only thing is, you probably don't know you have to follow an online procedure," he says, while beckoning me to follow him to his office.

"I wanted to deliver it in person; as for the official communication, I have already forwarded it online," I reply, faking a competence that I don't really possess. It was Domenico who informed me about the procedure, and he himself managed to submit my request by computer.

"By the way," I then add, "I would like to waive the notice period… so I'm resigning with immediate effect."

While we sit at his desk, I notice that he sounds bitter at my last remark and I can understand that: he would give his own eye-teeth to get up and quit himself.

"You know, it wasn't an easy decision, but I've made it; and I want to avoid any afterthought," I say, to appease him.

"I certainly understand," he says, with a pensive attitude, while looking at his computer.

"By your data, however, I understand that you won't be able to cash in your pension for a year-and-a-half, under the current laws. Are you aware of this?"

"Yes, thank you, I'm aware of that. But I have saved enough money in all these years, and I can handle things until the scheduled date."

"By the way, I didn't know you have a diploma from the Academy of Fine Arts; I've just realized that right now by scrolling through your file. Had I imagined that, I'd have offered you a career advancement years ago," he says in an apologetic tone.

Oh, my goodness, I think to myself, *after thirty-seven years of daily toilet-cleaning, what better moment to find out I've missed out on a promotion?*

"Thank you, I'm just fine with that," I reply.

As I leave the Ministry headed to my bank, I think back to my farewell with Reggi, who in the end wanted even to hug me.

"Well, I suppose you'll have a lot of spare time on your hands," he had suggested, in a mellifluous tone, leaving the sentence open-ended.

I looked at him aghast. I couldn't believe that this man, after ignoring me as a worker and a human being for almost four decades, was now proposing himself as my seducer.

"Honestly, I won't have spare time at all," I replied, refusing even to countenance his flirtations. "On Thursday I'm going to begin a home-care course for the terminally ill; I'll be starting volunteering in two weeks' time," I said.

Now, as I enter my bank for the last errand of the morning, I walk past the reception desk and go straight to my financial adviser's cubicle. Cosimo, at least, is as emotional as an ATM, and, given his discretion, he wouldn't bat an eye at me wearing a majorette uniform and fins on my feet.

Sitting in Cosimo's place—to my surprise—I find a dressy woman in her fifties—blonde and over-tanned. She invites me to sit down, explaining that Cosimo is on leave and that she has been summoned from another branch to replace him.

"Would you please tell me your full name?" the woman asks, her hands on the computer keyboard.

As I sit down before her, it's as if an invisible hand, a superhuman power, were tearing off me, one by one, backward, every day of my recent life, every minute of newfound confidence, every second of regained hope, every instant of my newborn serenity. A ruthless raid, a lacerating spoliation, behind which begins to emerge the withered nudity of yesterday's Vittoria: her cringing submissiveness, her acrimony and intolerance. The Vittoria I used to be before I started fighting, hoping, believing.

Before Nadine.

"Your full name please?" the woman repeats, leaning towards me her floral chiffon blouse: flamboyant, tacky, and off-season.

I try to avert my gaze from her, and it costs me such an effort that when I finally succeed, I take it as a first germ of rebellion.

"Vittoria Armieri," I answer in a choked voice, my gaze low. I know that chasing away the wave of suggestions won't be enough this time. This is too violent an upsurge. It's the response of an illness that refuses to go quietly.

My eyes still low on my black coat, I try to cling to a train of thought that drags me away from this vortex of negativity. I feel I have to start again from Nadine, and then through her, tenaciously, to recapture all of my stolen goods: to retrieve hope, to regain confidence, to recover serenity.

What is it that Nadine says? *Will wins over everything.*

And my will is to win.

Yes, I do want to win.

I most certainly do.

The woman's voice breaks my inner mantra, asking me, in a cold professional tone, to show her my ID.

"We do this for security reasons, in your own interest, Mrs. Armieri."

Head down, avoiding looking in her direction, I take out my ID card from my bag and hand it to her.

I want to win against my illness.

I want to win against that flowery blouse.

Against this woman's stormy past.

I want to prevail upon her damnations.

Which I don't even want to know.

Which I want out of my life.

She's there, in front of me; I can hear her tapping on the keyboard. Her presence is the wave itself, and it's against this latter that I must fight.

I know what I want.

And all the things I want, I want to see them before my eyes, the moment I think about them.

I want a home by the sea

I am able to get a glimpse of this house: it's white, flooded with sunlight, with a flowering jasmine that climbs between the wall and the rock. From inside, someone's about to open the shutters.

And inside this house I want Nadine

Now, there's Nadine looking out to the balcony, with her dark blouse and a radiant smile, while her face glows with the reflections of the sea.

I want her to be happy

A young, handsome man joins Nadine on the balcony; crossing his arms around her waist, he hugs her tenderly.

I want both of them to be happy

There's a little girl: she must be three years old; she has the same complexion as Nadine and her father's dark hair. He now takes her in his arms.

I want us all to be happy.

Nadine smiles and waves her hand to greet someone. She's greeting someone who is further down, under the balcony. She is immediately imitated by the man and the child.

I don't see to whom they're saying goodbye; I don't need to. It's clear who it is that they're bidding farewell.

This is the future I want to happen.

Now I can open my eyes and see again.

The woman has stopped tapping at her computer and is getting up from her seat.

No flashes come from her anymore.

None.

"Wait a moment, please, I'll be right back," she says, walking away.

I made it, I made it! I rejoice within myself.

And if I made it now, perhaps I can make it again.

My will has won.

Nadine has won.

The fate that brought us together has won.

Sitting in this cubicle, in front of an empty desk, I exult in my achievement. I praise that young and happy family, of which I hope one day I'll feel part.

"Mrs. Armieri," I suddenly hear.

But it's a male voice, and it's coming from behind me.

Passing me by, a burly man goes to sit in the empty chair.

"I am Carniti, the bank manager. Forgive my asking: are you Mrs. Vittoria Armieri?"

"Yes, that's right," I say, looking over at his dark suit.

"Would you please tell me the reason for your visit today?" he asks me, squinting in my direction.

"Of course, I'm here to unlock three hundred thousand euros from my investments," I say, glad to finally get to the point. "And, if possible, I would like them transferred to my bank account by Friday," I conclude.

Mr. Carniti looks away for a moment. Then, turning his gaze back to me, he pushes forward his torso. His words come out harsh and meticulous, almost brutal, as if he were announcing the charge of a prosecution.

"Look, there have been several suspicious movements on this account over these last few days. On Saturday alone, more than three thousand euros were spent in various boutiques in the center: that's the equivalent of the expenditure from this account across a seven-month period. Another two-hundred-and-fifty euros went on restaurants and taxis, plus five hundred euros taken from the ATM, and, finally, a cheque for seven hundred euros was issued in a jewelry store in Via del Corso…"

"That was for a pendant; Nadine was going to dine with Dr. Conetrali, and I wanted her to make a good impression."

My interruption seems to irk him even more, though.

"I don't know who Nadine and this Dr. Conetrali are. I know, however, that my colleague has found a discrepancy between the photo on your ID and your current appearance, as I can now appreciate myself. Moreover, she has noticed an attitude, on your part, that to call suspicious would be an understatement. Finally, you now want three hundred thousand euros to be unlocked by Friday. Now, you listen to me, please: before I'm forced to call the police, let me ask you one last time: are you Mrs. Vittoria Armieri?"

To his words I remain mute, motionless.

But it's not because I'm astounded that I delay responding. I'm just taking a pause for reflection.

What I'm about to say will get me into trouble, I know.

But I also know that today is a great day for me, so I have to celebrate it in a memorable way.

"Once again, are you or are you not Mrs. Vittoria Armieri? Just answer yes or no, please," he repeats, his patience now spent.

"I *am* Vittoria Armieri," I answer, with all calmness, "… and at the same time, *I'm not*," I add, defying his gaze.

The manager clenches his jaw and shakes his forefinger in front of my face, like a silent threat. Then, that same forefinger runs to the phone on the desk and begins to dial a number.

While I start sniggering to myself, silently, I am already looking forward to more expansive peals of delight from my Nadine.

THIRTY-SEVEN

More than seven months have passed since I met Nadine, and I often find myself reviewing them all. Sometimes, I even retrace those days one by one. I can thus relish the events that, taking me by the hand, made me the woman I am today.

Right now, it's a late afternoon in mid-June, and I'm sitting on a waterfront bench, one of the many dotted along this stretch of coast. Before my eyes, the promenade extends, all lined with lindens. Their rich foliage splashes with light-green shadows, at regular intervals, the deep blue of the sea. At the same time, it filters the exuberance of the sunset, as stunning as it is blinding. At this moment, I feel a thousand miles away from the bench at Villa Borghese, where I was sitting at the beginning of this story. Probably, not so much because the view has changed, but because of the transformation of this viewer.

I'm observing the families—the early birds of this summer season—as they slowly walk by. They arrive in dribs and drabs, with a swinging gait that reflects the breathing of the sea. Holding their children's hands, or just embracing each other, they stroll carefree; or, at least, so it seems to me.

An elderly man is sitting on the bench next to mine, a cap on his head and his right hand leaning on his stick. It seems that he's also absorbed by the holidaymakers' parade, but no one can tell that with certainty. He tilts his head slowly, following their steps; then, as if he were caught by a sudden memory, he returns his gaze to the horizon. Judging by his blotched and wrinkled face, he must be at least twenty years older than me. His hands,

221

knobbly and withered, suggest a past of hard work in a factory, or on a farm. And to think that—only eight months ago—I'd have already been into his life with all my being at the mere sight of him. Rather than just roughly guessing his age and his past occupation, I could have sworn to the day of his birth and every turn of his existence—every last step of it. In just a matter of seconds, all his moments of despair, his disappointments and the sufferings of his entire life would have already been absorbed into my sphere of emotions—transferred into my consciousness with such pain as to leave me shaken and exhausted. Now, instead, I know nothing about him; and I'm as good as ever. Observing him, right now, I rejoice at seeing nothing but an old man with a serene look on his face. His secrets of the past, which he may have shared with people now gone, are currently what they ought to be—just secrets.

Still, Nadine was right: it's not easy. There is no such thing as a magic bullet capable of returning me to normality. Today, I have replaced my illness with a relentless fight against it. Instead of giving in to my pain, I suffer from my strenuous battle. It's no less exhausting, but it makes me feel my life in my hands. Nadine has prescribed me her meds, and I must take them with stifling regularity. They are not drugs, fortunately, but rules, ploys, and codes to which I have to stick. None of these, in itself, can do anything against my illness; they are effective only in perfect unison, provided that I thoroughly respect the directions for use.

I open my handbag and pull out a sheet of paper folded in four. I carefully open it and lay it on my knees, trying to smooth its creases. Although I execute this last operation every time— or possibly just because of it—this sheet of paper is getting more and more wrinkled and yellowed. Nadine says that it's not enough for me to know its content by heart. She says that I must read it every day, dwelling on its every point. *It's part of the therapy*, she says. I put on my glasses and go through Nadine's harmonious script, where each letter seems to be designed with mathematical precision, as if it were measured with a caliber.

1. *The will always wins, but remember that to command your will, you must have the will to do so.*
2. *Cultivating a passion means never being in love enough with it. And you're never enough in love with a passion.*
3. *If you feel that an external emotion is going to overwhelm you, it's only because you haven't been able to find a stronger one within.*
4. *Love the lives of others: it's not their fault if they invade yours.*
5. *Escape the comfort of solitude: challenge yourself to be among people, more and more every day.*
6. *Dress dark, wear sunglasses, but color your inner life: laugh, play, joke, have fun.*
7. *Whatever dream—or nightmare—you may have at night, try to condense it into an image. Then, paint it using as many colors as you can.*
8. *Love, and then love again. And when you think you're done with loving, just think that you haven't started yet.*
9. *In short, to be clear, do the exact opposite of all you have done so far.*
10. *Ring me at least once a day. Today, for example, have you already called me?*

I take off my reading glasses, fold the paper into four once again and replace them both inside my handbag. From the next compartment, I pull out my phone. Another change in my life, one of many, is that I'm finally learning to use this gizmo properly. For example, my most recent progress is as follows.

"Call Nadine," I say, after pressing the command button.

While hearing the first ring, I notice that the old man next to me is now getting up, struggling to heave himself up onto the stick. As he shuffles towards the promenade, I think of the goodness of his heart; and I put aside the thought that, as with every human being, not all his life has been composed of good deeds.

"I love you, dear old man," is the whisper that I turn to him, as light as if it were a caress.

"Hello, Vicky! Are you finally here?" Nadine's voice asks, from the other end.

"Yes, I'm right here on the promenade. Domenico went to park the car and should join me in a minute."

"I can't wait for all of us to meet at dinner tonight."

"Same here, Nadine. Take your time, anyhow; there's no rush."

"I'll leave from here in half an hour, I'll be with you no later than seven-thirty."

After hanging up, I raise my eyes and go back to watching the slow amble along the promenade. I dwell on these silhouettes that at times exclude the farthest horizon from my view. I enjoy being free of their troubles and losing myself in the thoughts that please me the most.

And then, speaking about my thoughts, I now turn them to you, dear reader—you who have followed me all the way here. At this point, I can easily guess what you're expecting to happen.

Perhaps you'd like to know what Domenico has become to me—whether we have just remained friends or something else is growing between us. You may also be curious about Nadine: did I carry through my idea of adopting her, in the end? And what about the house here at Marina di Pisa, the one I bought last March? Did I register it in her name, as was my intention? Not to mention Nadine and Amedeo. It's plausible that you want to know whether they fell in love. You may also want to know whether they're having dinner with us tonight, and whether they plan to live together—maybe with the idea of having a child. These are all legitimate curiosities, and I understand them.

But I've spent too much time snooping around people's lives, for not respecting, and protecting, their privacy, now.

And, by the way, I have a question for you.

Why struggle to know things—events, lives—when nothing is more enthralling than trying to imagine them? You already know all that was important to know. Now it's time to put your fantasy at work, dear reader.

Keep imagining.
Isn't imagination, after all, what makes life worthwhile?

The end

Acknowledgments

Writing a novel in English as a non-native speaker may indeed be a curse. In fact, not unlike Vittoria (the protagonist of this story), I have had my moments of bleak despair. And again, not unlike her, I have overcome them through friendship and love. Old friends and new acquaintances, together with the professionals that I met during this journey, have helped me meet my goal. In this regard, the first person I want to thank is Anna Chávez; without her priceless work of editing, this book would have never seen the light. In the same spirit, I owe a special thanks to my dear friends Ash Tarhuni and Angus Mitchell. I'm not less thankful to all the other people who have always encouraged my activity as a writer, regardless of the language: first of all, my wife Patrizia and my mother, but also my two kids Federica and Riccardo. For their insightful comments, I especially thank Andrew Lawford, Gae Testa, Elena Camparada, Nicoletta and Alessandro Cernuto, Giuseppe Costa, Giuseppina Ortega and Daniel Bergamini. Finally, I want to extend my gratitude to my business partner Barbara Arioli, and to Roberto Pizzigoni, creative partner of my entire professional life. Without his approval of this story, there would have been no *Curse of Knowing*, but just a plot doomed to oblivion.

About the author

Aldo Cernuto (Turin, January 1955) lives between Camogli, on the Ligurian coast of Italy, and London. Copywriter and then executive creative director across some of the major advertising networks, he is now entirely devoted to writing novels.